What is
Hidden Bk.3
series

the FAIREST POISON

LAUREN SKIDMORE

the FAIREST POISON

SWEETWATER BOOKS
AN IMPRINT OF CEDAR FORT, INC.
SPRINGVILLE, UTAH

This is a work of fiction. The characters, names, incidents, places, and dialogue are products of the author's imagination, and are not to be construed as real. The opinions and views expressed herein belong solely to the author and do not necessarily represent the opinions or views of Cedar Fort, Inc. Permission for the use of sources, graphics, and photos is also solely the responsibility of the author.

ISBN 13: 978-1-4621-1792-5

Library of Congress Cataloging-in-Publication data on file

Published by Sweetwater Books, an imprint of Cedar Fort, Inc.
2373 W. 700 S., Springville, UT 84663
Distributed by Cedar Fort, Inc., www.cedarfort.com

Cover design by Michelle May Ledezma
Cover design © 2016 Cedar Fort, Inc.
Edited and typeset by Melissa J. Caldwell

Printed in the United States of America

10 9 8 7 6 5 4 3 2 1

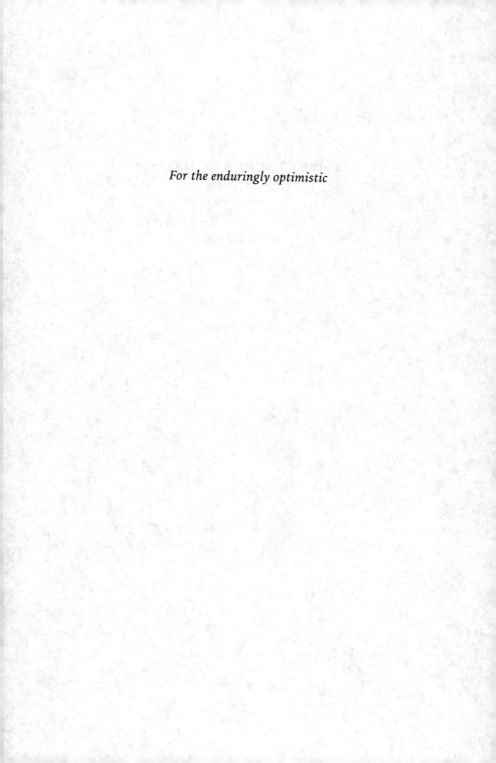

For the enduringly optimistic

ALSO BY LAUREN SKIDMORE

What Is Hidden
What Is Lost

Chapter One

My parents were sick.

That was the first news I received when I returned to the palace after nearly six months away. I was Venesia's princess, and so its ambassador. I was happy to serve . . . but not if it meant coming home to this.

"What's wrong?" I asked, shedding my cloak and shaking it out before handing it to a servant, still damp. It was still damp with seawater from the journey. It hadn't exactly been a peaceful trip. "Are they up to visitors now?"

The two handmaidens that had greeted me exchanged glances. "You should rest from your journey first, princess. It's late, and the details can wait until the morning."

I frowned. "No. You cannot welcome me back by saying my return may aid my parents' recovery and then refuse to tell me what's wrong."

"We don't want to worry you, princess," the other one said, throwing a nervous glance at her companion. She'd been with the palace longer and knew I would not be easily dissuaded from getting what I wanted.

"It's too late for that." I sighed. "Where is my brother?"

"Prince Aiden went to speak to the Guard about the successful capture of that Chameleon. He was eager to see the killer in person."

I braced myself. Aiden was in for a surprise on that front. "Maybe I will go rest after all," I said, brushing a dark curl behind my ear and adjusting the purple mask I wore across the upper half of my face. I would miss the freedom of not wearing my full Venesian mask while

I was away from court. "But don't think it's because you dissuaded me from seeing the king and queen tonight. Surely, if they were seriously ill, they'd have ordered you to take me to them right away. I won't disturb their sleep."

"Of course, princess." They both curtseyed.

"Bianca!"

I cringed. *Aiden.*

"You're dismissed," I said quickly to my handmaidens. I didn't need spectators for this.

They scurried away—though I'm sure to only just around the corner so they could eavesdrop—and I turned to face my elder brother.

He came barreling down the dimly lit corridor, his half-cloak billowing out behind him. He wore the emerald green mask he favored when he was out of the palace so no one would bother him as the prince. The pure white masks of the royal family tend to stand out in a sea of blues and green.

"Where is he?" he demanded. The head guard and a young woman in a green mask were just a few steps behind him. Looks like we were going to have an audience after all.

I was tempted to play dumb but knew that would only make him even more upset. And he had good reason to be upset; I couldn't deny him that.

"Please hear me out," I began slowly, my voice even and calm.

"You set him free, didn't you?" He shook his head in disbelief. "Bianca, he killed Evie's father." He gestured to the woman behind him, who shifted her weight from foot to foot uncomfortably, a medium-sized brown dog with a fluffy, curled tail at her heels. "He tried to kill me."

"I know that, but—"

"There is no excuse here! He killed and was willing to kill again. He stole masks and identities. He betrayed the trust of a kingdom who took him in. He is a criminal who needs to pay for his crimes."

"He saved my life. I owe him," I explained simply.

That made Aiden pause, but only for the length of a breath before retorting, "One good act does not make up for all the evil he's done."

"But it proves there is good in him."

"Or he is just trying to save his own skin by having you in his debt."

"He's not as terrible as you think he is."

"But you admit he is terrible."

"Aiden." I started to truly feel the late hour now and my shoulders drooped. "He deserves a fair trial at the very least."

"I can't give him a trial if he is mysteriously set free in the middle of the night."

"You're being dramatic."

"I think I'm being understandably upset. I went from news of my baby sister returning home with the scum I've been hunting for the past three months—to finding out that the scum has vanished and has said sister to thank for it! With everything that's been going on in court, and now with Mother and Father ill—"

"Do you know what's wrong with them?" I interrupted, both wanting to know and hoping to change the subject. I'd bristled slightly at being called his "baby sister"—there were only two years between us, after all—but was willing to overlook it in the name of the greater good of the moment. His accusations weren't untrue; he just didn't know the Chameleon like I did.

I might have been part of the reason he'd been captured, but we had a history. And that history meant that I owed him his freedom.

It seemed Aiden was as tired of arguing as I was. He answered, "The doctors aren't sure. It's not an illness they're familiar with. Mother and Father are on bed rest now until a cure can be found. They can barely eat and are very weak, and they both have a pink rash all over their bodies. It happened so suddenly, but no one else in court has the same symptoms, so we don't know where it came from."

"How long have they been like this? Why did no one tell me?"

"They only just felt sick enough to admit it and seek a doctor, though Father mentioned to me he'd been feeling poorly for several days."

I sighed. It was just like them to overlook any health problems until they got too serious to ignore. They didn't want to appear weak in front of the kingdom, and to appear human was to appear weak. In the king's eyes, at least.

"I'll go see them first thing in the morning. We all need our rest." I gave Aiden a meaning- ful look. "That means you as well." I was sure his mask hid dark circles under his eyes, one benefit of our country's tradition. I knew my brother, and he'd been pushing himself too hard. I'd gotten snippets of the unrest that had crept into our court from his letters while I was away, but it was another matter to see him in person.

From what I understood, the court was reluctant to accept him as their next ruler. He had no respect for tradition, they claimed. For generations, the royal family protected them- selves behind pure white masks, fine clothes, and strict rules. Aiden wanted to make changes that gave him more personal freedom as well as control over the country.

"We'll all of us go to sleep, and discuss things again after breakfast."

"Fine," he begrudged as he turned, offering his arm to the woman beside him, who looked as tired as I felt, plus awkward after witness- ing a royal argument. Evie, he said her name was. He'd written about her. He had proposed marriage to her, and she'd said no.

I was very curious about her.

"I am glad you're home, though. I missed you," he said.

I smiled. "I missed you too." My gaze shifted to Evie, and I opened my mouth to greet her properly.

"Let's save introductions for a less unconventional time," he interrupted before I could say anything. He reached for her hand, tucking it in the crook of his arm. "I'd rather your official meeting be a more pleasant one. Or at least one where we're not arguing."

She rolled her eyes at him but offered me a shy smile.

"If you insist," I replied with a smile for her and a raised eyebrow for him. Its effect was somewhat lessened thanks to my mask, but he knew my expressions well enough to spot it.

He chuckled and shook his head with affection in his eyes. "Until tomorrow," he said, and we parted ways.

The halls were dim and quiet, but I could have found my way to my chambers in the dark. I rarely left the palace growing up, and walking through these halls now felt like slipping into a warm bath. I loved the palace.

Servants had already brought my trunk to my parlor. Normally, I would need help dressing for bed, thanks to the complex finery of the clothing that comes with royalty, but since I was still dressed in a simple traveling dress, I didn't bother ringing for a handmaiden.

I'd missed my rooms. It had been a long time since I'd been alone, and my rooms were the one place I was granted my privacy. For six months, I'd been acting as ambassador to Nishima, a neighboring country we had strong ties with. That meant that for nearly six months, I'd been constantly surrounded by people—if not by the dignitaries I was there to see, then by my own guards who never left my side. Even on the journey home, when we'd been sidetracked by the hunt for the Chameleon, I'd never been left on my own.

But in my own palace, in my own rooms, I was alone. And I felt safe.

I fell asleep almost as soon as my head touched my pillow.

The next morning, I'd barely dressed before I heard insistent knocks at the doors to my suite. I knew it was Aiden even before my handmaiden opened the door to reveal him.

"I said after breakfast, Aiden. I'm still—"

"They've gotten worse," he interrupted me, his eyes grim. "Mother and Father. And another doctor, a specialist from Nishima, has examined them."

He opened and closed his mouth several times, searching for the right words.

"Just say it. What is it?"

"Bianca . . . they've been poisoned."

Chapter Two

"oison? You're sure?" I reached out to him, and he caught my arm, steadying me as I swayed.

He nodded, his expression grim. "The physician says he's seen it before. But it's not all bad news. He says he knows the antidote."

I exhaled but couldn't relax just yet. "That's good news. Why do you still look so worried?"

"Many reasons. Let me take you to see them, and I'll explain there."

He didn't speak as we hurried through the palace, and I knew better than to ask him anything. One of the first lessons we learned as children was that the walls have ears, and those ears are not always friendly. Growing up, I learned to assume every word I spoke could be heard by an enemy.

It seemed Aiden had finally learned that lesson as well.

He was forever sneaking out of the palace, abandoning his lessons and causing our parents no small amount of grief. Watching him now, I could see a change in him. He carried himself differently. Something in the confidence of his step and in the heavy angle of his shoulders.

He'd grown up while I'd been away.

We reached the royal bedchambers quickly, and after a quick word from Aiden to the guards stationed outside the wide, gold-enameled doors, we entered my parents' antechamber.

I was hit with a wave of incense, the heavy scent of sandalwood and almonds making my eyes water. Aiden coughed, raising a gloved hand to shield his nose. He spotted the physician immediately and demanded, "What is that?"

"Medicine, my prince," the physician responded quickly. He was a tall, reedy man, though my brother still had several inches on him. He wore a scarlet red mask rimmed in silver and gold, with seeing glasses built into the eyeholes. "Princess," he greeted me with a solemn bow. He spoke softly, and I could see through the door to the bedchambers that the curtains around my parents' bed were closed. They must be sleeping.

"Dr. Hayashia, my sister, Princess Bianca." Aiden quickly waved off the introductions. "How can they even breathe in here?" he asked with a skeptical glance at the windows, which were covered with sapphire-blue velvet curtains.

"It is part of the antidote, my prince." Dr. Hayashia's eyes flickered between my brother's and mine as Aiden started to pace the room.

"Is the antidote to smother them?" he murmured.

"O-of course not, my prince. Please sit, both of you, and I will explain while we wait for them to wake."

"I want to see them first," I spoke up. "Just for a moment."

The doctor jumped at my voice. I couldn't fault him for being startled—a long-standing tradition in Venesia declared that royal voices could only be heard by a select few called Speakers, who would then relay our commands. The current Speaker, a tall, dark-skinned woman called Vanna was a familiar companion with a beautiful voice, and she spent more time with the royal family than anyone. I was surprised I hadn't seen her yet, but I knew that for the sake of convenience, this rule was more relaxed inside the palace walls—especially since Aiden had stepped into power. If the doctor were new to the palace, though, he wouldn't know how we do things here.

"Of course, princess, but truly—just a moment. They are still very ill."

I stepped inside the bedchamber. I rarely visited this room, even as a child. The strongest memory I had of it was the last time my mother had been sick. I was still a child, not even into my mask yet, so she'd indulged me when I begged to visit her. It had been during a particularly cold winter, and she'd insisted she was fine. My father pretended to believe her until she fainted during a dinner procession. After that, she agreed to rest. I would read my history lessons to her, and she would help me practice my Nishimi. Had I been older than twelve, old enough to have proven myself deserving of my white mask, I doubt I would have been allowed. It wouldn't have been appropriate, though I still didn't quite understand why.

Then, the warm room had been welcoming; now, it was suffocating. I drew back the curtain, peering into the darkness. I could barely make out their pale faces.

I let the curtain fall. I didn't want to see them like this. I didn't want to hear their labored breathing. They were the king and queen of Venesia. They should be standing strong and proud.

I joined my brother, slipping my hand into the crook of his arm for support.

"I want to know everything about this poison," he was saying.

"It looks to be the work of a strand of poison ivy called Demon's Hair. The leaves alone are poisonous but not fatal. However, crushing the leaves, mixing them with sap from the vine, and allowing the mixture to ferment can create something much stronger. Contact with the plant usually only causes the rashes with some irritation, but Their Highnesses have had a strong reaction. Either they were exposed to a very potent mixture or their bodies are naturally more sensitive than most. The ivy grows wild in the forest, though I do not know where."

"So not difficult to acquire?"

"No, my prince. It would just take a little patience to find."

"And not fatal?"

"Very rarely. I expect Their Highnesses to recover fully in a few weeks' time."

Aiden frowned. "I'd like to speak with my sister. I'm sure you're hungry and could use a reprieve. We'll send for you if anything changes or if we need your assistance."

"Thank you, my prince."

The door had barely closed before Aiden pulled away from me to begin pacing again, one hand brushing his hair out of his eyes.

"What are you thinking?" I asked softly, knowing his expression too well.

"It couldn't have been an accident, with a poison that takes such deliberation to make. And it couldn't have been a spur-of-the-moment action. Someone—" He sighed and looked at me.

"But the doctor said it was rarely fatal."

"That's what I don't understand," he said, his frown deepening. "Why go to such trouble if not to complete the deed?"

"Have the nobles been acting up while I was away?"

He stopped pacing to drop into a plush armchair. " 'Acting up' would be putting it nicely. Ever since the Chameleon attacks, families have been suspicious of each other." I stiffened at the Chameleon's name, which Aiden raised an eyebrow at but didn't comment on. "And it didn't help that I chose Evie, a commoner, at my masquerade instead of someone from a noble family. They don't know where the power will shift once I marry, and it makes them nervous. They've been pressuring me to make another choice. Hold another ball, even, as if that would change my mind."

"Marry?"

"Yes, marry, believe it or not," he said, chuckling. "But that's also rather complicated at the moment, and it's so stuffy in here I can barely think, let alone explain that right now."

"You gave her an awful first impression of me."

"That was your own fault. And since we keep coming back to this, we really do need to discuss the Chameleon." His expression darkened. "But I don't want to do it here. My head is starting to hurt."

Mine was as well, and I breathed a sigh of relief at the stay of execution.

"We'll eat, then get this over with." He rose to his feet with a groan. "We've both got a busy day. Dinner will be quite an affair tonight to celebrate your return."

"Thanks," I said dryly. "You know how I love a spectacle."

He laughed, tapping the underside of my chin with affection. "That's how you know you're home. Everything's a spectacle here."

I returned to my own chambers, opening my windows wide to let in the fresh air. Spring was reluctant to arrive this year, so it was still chilly, but the brisk air felt wonderful after being confined in that suffocating room. Not wanting to return to court quite yet, I ordered a tray to be sent up, and before long a handmaiden was setting out my breakfast.

Even when I dined in public in Venesia, I would be behind a screen, so it made little difference. I wanted to eat without having to worry about my mask and took my meals in my room whenever possible. Growing up, I would often dine with Aiden, but the older he grew, the more likely he was to be missing or out getting into trouble.

So I wasn't unfamiliar with dining without company, but it had been a long time. As I spread grape jam across a pastry, I realized

I was actually lonely. I'd grown too used to dining with my guards while I was traveling.

I made plans to visit them soon—two were recovering from injuries from our journey, and the others had been granted a few days' leave before returning to my side. I didn't need personal guards in the palace.

At least, I hadn't in the past. Knowing my brother, that might change soon.

An unfamiliar knock sounded at my door, and I rose as a handmaiden moved to open it.

"Hello, princess," the young woman said. *Evie,* I reminded myself. My brother's intended. Sort of. "I'd hoped I'd find you here."

"Please, come in," I said quickly. "I'm just finishing. Are you hungry?"

"No, I ate with Aiden. But he ate so quickly I'd barely said a sentence before he was done and on his feet again, off to meet with some noble so-and-so." She made a distinctly unladylike sound of disapproval in her throat, endearing herself to me immediately. "Do you mind if Hachi comes in as well?" The little dog's ears perked up at his name.

"Of course not, please." I wagged my

fingers at him, but he seemed more interested in sniffing the furniture and walls. Aiden had mentioned the dog, how he was one of the few things from her former life she was able to hold on to and how he made her feel a little safer after everything she'd been through. "As for Aiden," I said fondly, "he does that. And he hated how slowly I would eat. Whenever we dined in court, he couldn't leave until I was done, so I would eat as slow as possible to annoy him."

She laughed and gave me an appraising smile. "He said I would like you."

"He's not had much time to tell me about you, but he mentioned you in letters. I look forward to getting to know you better."

"I'm still getting to know myself here as well," she confessed. "Life in the palace is exhausting." She told me how she split her time between studying under a master in the Masking Rooms and studying everything else with Aiden. She was a skilled mask-maker and hadn't wanted to give it up, but as the girl chosen by the prince at the masquerade ball, she had certain obligations.

"I don't know how you grew up with all of this. Aiden said you never snuck away like he did."

I shrugged one shoulder. "Someone had to be the responsible one."

Speaking of responsibilities, it was time to meet Aiden to discuss my latest endeavor. I sobered as I remember what the Chameleon had done to the girl in front of me.

As much as I believed in him now, there was no denying the fact that he'd done terrible things in the past. He stole masks and impersonated the owners, which is where the nickname came from, and Evie and her father had been two of his victims. The Chameleon had killed Evie's father as he stole his mask and branded Evie with a Mark in an attempt to frame her. Marks were undeniable brands on the faces of criminals and those we didn't want to disappear behind a mask. The scars could be hidden but never erased.

Even Aiden had a moment of doubt at the sight of her Mark.

"I never told you I was sorry for what happened to you."

She looked down at her hands. "Thank you."

"Aiden probably doesn't want me to talk to you about it, but I think you have a right to know."

She shook her head and stood abruptly. "I don't want to know. I understand what you're trying to do, but I don't want to talk about him."

I bit my bottom lip, disappointed in myself for ending our first meeting on such a sour note. For my brother's sake, I wanted her to like me. And, so far, I liked her. If she married Aiden, we'd be social equals—a rare opportunity for a friend for me.

I apologized, but she just gave me a sad smile. "I should be going. I have work to do. Good luck with Aiden."

"Please feel free to visit me again," I said, a weight settling on my chest as I felt her close herself off to me.

She summoned Hachi to her, then curtseyed at the door before she disappeared. Polite, but distant. That meeting hadn't gone as well as I had hoped, and I resolved to get to know her better before the engagement was official.

Sighing, I turned to don a new mask to meet my brother.

We had a secret place, the two of us, where we could meet without fear of being over-heard. We'd wear the masks and clothes of nobles or servants—anything but the pure, easily stained white of royalty—and slip away to the forest and the tiny hidden room.

The entrance was built into a thick oak tree trunk, with stairs spiraling down to the underground room. It was dark and musty, and I carefully lit the lantern we kept on the top step before closing the camouflaged door behind me and descending.

There wasn't room for much, but I could stand and move around comfortably. As I hung the lantern on a hook in the ceiling, I noticed stacks of papers scattered around the room: one on the worn wooden chair I'd always favored, another two on a small side table next to the chair that had always been Aiden's, and several more lining the wall. A stack of thick books sat at the feet of the other chair as well, bookmarked with scraps of paper.

All Aiden's, of course. Why he'd work here instead of somewhere in the palace wasn't hard to guess, either. This place was built in secret by our great-grandfather and known only to the royal family. He wouldn't be disturbed as long as he worked here, though I'm sure he ruffled a few feathers when he disappeared.

I didn't have to wait long for him to join me.

"Mother and Father woke for a moment," he greeted me. I felt a pang of sadness in missing the opportunity to speak to them. "I told them you were back. They said they're glad you made it home safely, but regret not being able to welcome you back on better terms."

"I'll visit them again after dinner," I said. I didn't know how quickly they'd recover, but after a full day of breathing in the medicine, surely they'd show some progress at the end of the day.

He nodded his approval and lowered himself into his chair. The chairs in here were much less ornate, but they were comfortable. It was one of the rare places Aiden would actually sit still.

"So," he said, looking at me intently. "You think the Chameleon deserves a pardon."

Chapter Three

$\mathcal{I}$ knew Aiden was making an attempt to remain calm, but his stillness only made me more nervous. "I don't know," I said to try to ease my way into the difficult conversation gently. "I will grant you that I didn't experience his crimes the same way you did. I know it's personal for you."

He grunted his agreement.

"But I can also honestly tell you that he saved my life. And I know that you don't know the whole story. He was wronged as well."

"That's no excuse for what he did."

"Maybe not, but it's an explanation and something that needs to be taken into consideration."

"You don't understand, Bianca. I'm the acting regent right now. If they see any weakness in me, they will take advantage of me. I need to be seen as strong. I can't just let this go."

"You want to make an example of him," I said in a flat voice.

"I want to see justice served."

"Is this justice or revenge?"

"Justice." He sounded so sure of himself, but there was a flicker in his eyes. "For Evie."

I crossed my arms. "I won't try to stop you, but I won't help you in this."

"I don't need your help."

I flinched.

He saw and immediately stood to apologize. "I didn't mean that to come out so harsh."

"And yet."

For a moment, we just stared at each other, neither knowing quite what to say.

Maybe we'd been apart too long.

"I don't want to fight with you," I finally said, breaking the uncomfortable silence. "But I won't change my mind on this."

"And neither will I."

"Can we agree to focus on things here first? Figure out who's behind the poisoning. Keep everyone safe here and now before hunting down a threat that doesn't exist."

I could tell he wanted to argue, but he held his tongue. "Fine. One thing at a time."

He was reluctant to leave without talking of happier things, but he said there were too many things for him to do, especially with the new information about the poison. We both returned to the palace, and I spent the afternoon checking in on my injured guards and the general state of the palace. Like Aiden, I wore my royal whites as little as possible, since it was so much easier to talk and get information in the clothes of a noble.

But I couldn't put them off forever, and soon it was time to dress for dinner.

I needed two handmaidens to dress and

style my hair. One entered carrying a large basin of water.

"What's that for?"

"The newest fashion, princess," she explained. All the palace servants wore silver masks with their own unique markings, but I didn't recognize hers, and she was apparently too nervous to meet my eyes. I waited patiently for her to continue. "The fabric of the ribbons in your new corset needs to be soaked to make them easier to tie."

I fought to keep my face neutral. Every time I returned from overseas, I came back to another silly fashion trend. From Aiden's letters, I'd hoped this time would be the glass masks—a trend I could observe but never have to suffer through. It seemed I wasn't so lucky. "Very well," I sighed.

Thus began the ordeal of being smothered in fabric. First the shift, then the corset with its uncomfortably damp ribbon pulled tight. Then came the underskirt, and finally the gown itself.

The gown was beautiful but uncomfortable as I sat stiff as a board waiting for the other handmaiden to do my hair. This girl's mask I recognized, and she was quick to do her work, weaving strands of hair into elaborate braids. The look was completed as I donned the white mask that covered my face from chin to temple.

I always thought I looked like something of a ghost when I wore it, as it erased my sense of me completely. That was the point, naturally, but I'd never grown comfortable with it.

"All done, princess," the handmaiden said, tucking one last ribbon into place.

I could barely breathe, but I didn't dare voice my complaints to her. She had no power over the fashions, and I didn't want rumors spreading that I couldn't handle them.

I dismissed the pair of them, though it seemed the nervous one had already fled. *She won't last long here*, I thought sadly. The palace had no patience for those weakened by fear.

From that moment, dinner was much as I'd expected it to be, and I was already exhausted by the time I finally reached my seat.

"You seem out of breath; are you all right?" Aiden asked me once we were behind the privacy of the royal screen. The rest of court dined at long tables circling the room as we sat on a dais at the head. Heavy sapphire-blue velvet curtains hung behind us and on either side, with the wooden accordion screen at the front blocking us completely from view so we could eat without any part of our faces visible. The front of the screen was lovely, painted white with gold designs of scenes from Venesian canals, masks, and the royal seal: a crown and a long, thin blade. It also contained a patterned strip of strategically placed one-way glass along the top so we weren't blind to the court. They saw only mirrored glass, but we saw a window. It needed to be quite dark for us to see through clearly, which was one reason we used such thick curtains on the remaining sides.

"I'm fine," I said, waving his concerns aside. "Just more tired than I thought I was, I suppose." I quickly changed the subject, removing my mask and surveying the banquet of food laid out before us. "Where's Evie? Did you know she visited me earlier?"

His face softened at the mention of her name. "She doesn't like to dine in ceremony, and it's not fair to make her quite yet. I'm still easing her into all the pomp and circumstance. She's probably in the Masking Rooms, working on a new project."

For a moment, it was easy between us again. He asked me about my travels and some of the people I'd been sent to talk to, and I was happy to tell him about my success as an ambassador.

One of my favorite stories to share was one that began with my playing with a young Nishimi prince who couldn't have been more than five years old. He was clearly bored at the formal dinner, and we discovered that neither of us cared for the local specialty served—fermented soybeans.

"This adorable child and I had another thing in common," I said with a grin. "We both love dogs, apparently. He had two as near-constant companions."

"Well-fed companions, I'm sure."

I shrugged one shoulder. "I'm sure I wouldn't know."

Aiden groaned. "And that didn't endanger

your relationship with his parents? The very politically powerful people you were sent to impress?"

"Well, I don't think his father approved," I admitted, "but his mother laughed and laughed and then introduced me to several key court ladies the next evening, who then spoke favorably of me to their husbands, who then were useful counselors to the emperor when it came time to discuss import regulations. Plus, the dogs loved me."

"Well as long as the dogs love you."

I winked at him. Despite the sarcasm, I knew he was impressed. He had no patience for working out the inner relationships of court members. It was a good thing I was home again, because it looked like I would need to start working my magic in our own court to turn the people to his side.

My happiness was short lived, however, as it was starting to get more difficult to draw breath. It seemed like the corset was getting even tighter, and I was starting to feel dizzy.

"I want to check on Mother and Father before I retire for the night," I announced.

"Excellent; let's go." He'd already finished his meal, naturally.

We exited the dining hall through a secret corridor only the royal family had access to in order to avoid another grand processional. Another reason for curtains—they easily hid the doors we could escape through.

However, as long as we were in our whites, we might as well be in parade no matter where we walked. We both would have preferred to change before visiting our parents, but impatience won out over practicality.

We donned our full face masks again and slipped outside. Servants fluttered out of the way like leaves on the wind as we strode past, flattening against the walls with their heads bowed. Neither Aiden nor I spoke along the way.

I was lightly winded again by the time we reached the royal chambers, much to my annoyance, and the air was still cloyingly thick with incense. I coughed as we entered.

Aiden shot me a concerned look. "Are you sure—"

"Yes, I'm fine," I interrupted, a bit more

snappish than I'd meant. I was starting to feel light-headed.

He pressed his lips together but didn't say anything further, walking ahead of me to peek in our parents' bedroom. "Still sleeping," he reported, sounding disappointed.

"Sleeping isn't bad," I said.

"No, but I'm sure they would want to see you."

"I'll sit and wait here for a spell. Maybe they'll wake up for a moment." I wanted to rest a few minutes before returning to my own room anyway.

He looked torn. "I would wait with you, but Evie is expecting me. We usually meet in the evenings for 'courtly lessons,' as she calls them."

"Go," I urged him. "I'll be perfectly fine. Tell her hello for me."

He gave my arm an affectionate squeeze and slipped outside.

"My prince, I thought I would find you here," I heard Speaker Vanna call to him. I considered going out to greet her, but she had already whisked him away before I even reached the door. It seemed Evie would have to wait.

I lowered myself into an armchair, blinking, and tried to breathe as deeply as my corset would allow. Which is to say, not very deeply at all, and I couldn't relax my spine without the whalebone digging into my ribs.

The light-headedness was growing. This incense was choking me. I needed more air. I pushed my mask up, but that provided little relief.

The windows. Surely I could open them for just a moment without endangering my parents.

I shot to my feet.

I underestimated my dizziness.

As if I were watching from outside myself, I saw myself trip on the hem of my gown. I stumbled, the thick fabric tangling around my legs, and hit the ground hard.

Pain shot through my side, my ribs crashing against the hard boning of my blasted corset. I tried to right myself, but I was still too dizzy.

"I can't breathe," I whispered, and my eyes fluttered shut.

Chapter Four

I woke in my room, disoriented and surrounded by pillows. It was dark outside, but my room was lit by a small lantern on my bedside table. I shifted, trying to push some pillows away, and inhaled sharply at the pain in my right side.

"Bianca." Aiden was suddenly there, hovering over me, his face drawn in concern. "Careful. Are you okay?"

I gently pressed him back, and he sat in a chair that had been drawn near my bedside. I noticed a small stack of papers at the foot of my bed. I made an amused face—he'd been using my bed as a desk. "What happened?"

"Someone tried to kill you."

A nervous laugh escaped me and I winced. It hurt to laugh. "Be serious," I breathed, but he didn't seem to be in a joking mood.

He rose from the chair again, frowning. "I am serious. The ties on your corset were so tight that it was cutting off your breathing."

"That's a poor fashion decision, not an attempt on my life."

"When the material is designed to shrink as it dries, and you are laced up wet, you can't fault me for being suspicious."

"What do you know about ladies' fashion?"

Evie spoke up for the first time. I hadn't noticed her, but she stepped forward so I could see her more easily. "The laces aren't supposed to get wet. That kind of fabric caused so many injuries like yours when it was introduced to court that most ladies don't use it anymore."

"It wasn't an attack on me," I insisted. Aiden refused to listen or even sit down again.

"It must have been an accident. The girl probably grabbed the wrong laces."

"And accidentally soaked them in water?"

"Maybe she misunderstood something. I'm
sure if you ask her, she can clear this whole
thing up."

"The girl who did it is nowhere to be found.
That's not suspicious to you?"

It was, but I didn't want to give in. "She's
probably scared of what you'll do to her. It
was an accident," I insisted.

"The doctor said it bruised your ribs!" That
explained the dull pain with each breath.

"A bad accident," I amended. "But I'll
recover."

"We can't just brush this aside."

"I'm not saying we should, but—"

"I need to do something."

"You need to breathe. Trust me, I do not
recommend not breathing."

He gave me a dirty look. "Ha."

"Please at least sit," I asked again. "It must
be late, and you look tired."

"Forgive me for not looking my best after a
murder attempt on my sister," he grumbled as

he bent over the bed to shuffle his papers into a neat stack. Evie laid a hand on his shoulder and murmured something I couldn't hear before nodding a brief farewell to me. Aiden pouted as she left the room.

I sighed. He could be so dramatic.

"You're giving me a headache," I complained. "And I wish you wouldn't use my bed as a writing desk. You get ink everywhere."

"I had work to do. And you're not very interesting to be around when you sleep."

"You didn't have to stay here."

"Of course I did." He look offended. "What if someone tried attacking you while you were unconscious? What if the corset had done more damage than the doctor thought? What if—"

"All right, all right," I interrupted. I was glad he was there, but I knew him. He was dangerously close to going overboard with his protective measures. "You could have stationed guards outside my door and had a handmaiden inside to let you know when I woke up."

He shook his head. "I don't trust any of

your handmaidens after what happened. I'll be questioning them all in the morning."

"Carefully," I warned him. "You'll question them carefully. Don't let them see how frazzled you are."

"I'm not frazzled."

I gave him a hard look.

"I'm not," he repeated, not about to be cowed by his younger sister.

I'd believe him if we had any servants left after lunch.

"The doctor will see you in the morning to check your ribs. You're to stay in bed until he says otherwise."

I wanted to protest but honestly didn't feel much like moving. Some time in bed would probably be wise.

"I should let you go back to sleep. I'll send someone up with something to help with the pain. For now, you just need to rest and heal. You'll be back on your feet and causing trouble again in no time."

I smiled. "Thanks. I look forward to it."

The next morning, the doctor was optimistic but said I should take the day easy and

stay in bed, and while he would prefer I take
several more days to recuperate, bed rest
for any longer than that wouldn't be necessary as long as I was careful. I promised I
wouldn't do anything too strenuous, and that
was that.

As much as my ribs hurt, I was bored
almost instantly. As an ambassador, I was
constantly meeting with people, making con-
nections, and smoothing over snares. As I
traveled, I trained physically with my guards
so I wouldn't lose my edge—I'd been trained
to be my own best protector for as long as I
could remember.

Lying around in bed doing nothing was a
foreign concept to me.

The pain in my side had become a dull
throb after a special tea the doctor gave me,
and it was easy enough to ignore, as long as I
didn't laugh or breathe too deeply.

I didn't have many visitors, just the doctor
and a pair of guards who brought my breakfast. They reminded of the guards I'd traveled
with, and I made a note to check in on them
once I was on my feet again.

When Aiden came by in the afternoon, I found out why visitors were so scarce.

"How are you feeling?" he asked as he stood at the foot of my bed.

"Bored," I answered honestly. I'd caught up on letters and some reading, but it was only midafternoon, and I was anxious to get up and move. "And slightly abandoned. Where has everyone gone?"

A guilty look flashed across his face. "I couldn't have anyone in here that I didn't trust."

"So you dismissed everyone."

"Maybe."

"Aiden," I groaned.

"I need to check the history of all your servants before they're allowed anywhere near you. And you're not to go anywhere without at least one guard with you. Maybe two."

"Aiden," I repeated, but he ignored me.

"I would prefer you take your meals in private as well. In here, actually, since you need rest while your ribs heal. The less you move, the better, and the fewer opportunities for anything to take advantage of your state."

"Are you confining me to my rooms like a child?" I asked in disbelief, cutting him off from continuing what sounded to be a long list of restrictions. It was unbelievable, considering how many times I knew for a fact he climbed out of his windows to escape his obligations. He'd even been too old to be called a child the last time I remembered.

He paused only for a moment, then turned to give me a hard look. "It is my duty to protect you. So if that's what it takes, yes. And I'd appreciate it if you took your own safety more seriously."

I sighed. "Just call my usual guards back. I'd hoped to give them more time after our journey, but they'll do what you ask. Rufina and Carmine can act as my handmaidens; you liked them." I named two of my female guards, both proven fighters. Rufina was a tall, quiet one, but Carmine was excellent company. "And Doc would be a useful guard. Pair him with Ernesto and no one would get past them." Doc wasn't a practicing doctor—he wore the guard's black mask—but the nickname stuck after he patched me up several times. "That's four guards right there."

Aiden considered this and then sighed. "Fine. I'll ask for them to come as soon as they're able."

"Wonderful. And I'm not going to just sit here and do nothing, by the way. I was thinking that it'd be nice to introduce Evie to several of the noblewomen. I'm sure you've neglected that part of her 'courtly lessons,' am I right?"

"She said she didn't feel ready."

"Well, of course not, if you were going to make her do it on her own. But I'll be there. It will be good for both of you if she's less of a mystery. I'm sure the ladies are curious."

"I don't care about them."

I sighed. "You need to care, Aiden. You'll be their king."

He winced. "You know what I meant. I don't care what they think of her; it won't change my opinion."

"But you still need their approval, or at least their respect, or they'll turn against you."

"Fine. Have your tea party or whatever you decide to do. But do it guarded and keep it short."

"Tea sounds excellent, actually. I'll arrange that today."

"Wonderful," he grumbled. "Now if you don't mind, I have servants to track down."

I did mind, but I chose to keep my comments to myself when it was clear there was no dissuading him.

After he was gone, I went to work writing invitations to tea, carefully selecting ladies who would go easy on Evie. I was not close to any of them, but I remembered their personalities and quickly had a group of five ladies to invite. Adding Evie and myself to the count, the group was small enough to not be so intimidating, but large enough that I doubted conversation would lag. If this first meeting went well, I could slowly make my way through court until all the important players knew Aiden's intended.

With that complete, I was back to searching for some kind of amusement. Perhaps I would redecorate my sitting room. There was a large, gold-framed, full-length mirror I'd never particularly liked, but it had been there as long as I could remember. Maybe it was time I finally got rid of it and its twin in my bedroom.

Aiden burst into my room, interrupting my musing, and I knew instantly something had happened.

"Did you find her? The servant girl?"

"Yes."

Aiden wasted no time, calling for the full court to immediately convene in the throne room. Most trials were delegated to judges, but Aiden would, of course, see to this one personally.

He sat in his white robes, his face completely covered by a smooth white mask free of any decoration. The throne was white as well, high backed, with carvings of masks and waves expertly crafted into the woodwork.

He didn't look like Aiden when he sat there. He looked like a ghost, hungry for vengeance.

I sat near him in my own whites, my seat not a throne but still an elegant chair, feeling less like an avenging ghost and more like a drooping lily. I concentrated on my breathing, silently urging the pain in my side to go away.

The trial passed much like I expected and

was over quickly. The girl confessed her inexperience with a tearstained face. She claimed a noble told her wetting the lacings was the way things were done, but she couldn't name the lady.

It was clear to me that Aiden didn't believe her, though no emotion could be detected behind his stark mask.

In the past, in the rare occasions a member of the royal family presided over a trial in place of a judge, the Speaker would ask all questions as well as deliver the sentencing, but it seemed that was another tradition Aiden was doing away with. Vanna was nowhere to be seen, and the prince regent seemed to have no qualms over speaking for himself.

"I hereby declare you guilty of treason by endangering the life of a member of the royal family." Aiden's voice was steady and surprisingly calm. "You will be Marked, stripped of your mask, and exiled from Venesia."

The girl dropped to her knees, and black-masked guards immediately dragged her away.

The court broke into whispers as Aiden swiftly walked out of the room. I lingered for just a moment, wanting to gauge their reactions. This was the first time I'd seen Aiden as the prince regent since I'd returned, and as judge, the first time anyone had seen a member of the royal family personally conduct a trial in years.

Reactions seemed mixed, which worried me. If there were people confident enough to voice their disapproval here in court, they might be confident enough to do more than just talk.

I was careful to watch the ladies I intended to send invitations, too, as there was no doubt this topic would come up. Ladies Renata and Luciana were speaking rapidly to one another, but they looked more excited by the novelty of Aiden's presence, as they kept craning their necks at him, and I remembered they'd both idolized my brother when we were younger. It seemed they still admired him. Only one lady in particular really worried me, a Lady Mariana. I'd been nervous to include her in the first place because she could be quite judgmental, but I thought I'd be able to handle her. She looked visibly displeased at the way Aiden had handled things, a frown on her lips as she spoke only to her mother standing beside her.

I would need to address that.

Aiden and I dined in private. He didn't appear to be in a talkative mood, but once we were alone, I had to ask.

"Was all this really worth it?"

The coldness in his voice scared me as he answered.

"Yes."

Chapter Five

$\mathcal{I}$t didn't take long for me to discover what Aiden's safety measures truly entailed.

My familiar guards arrived the next morning, and I greeted them with a hug. As annoyed as I was with Aiden's overprotective nature, it was good to see them again. With as much time as we spent together while I traveled, and as often as they'd protected me from harm, it was always a comfort to have them near me. However, my happiness at seeing them didn't override my frustration at Aiden's insistence they were necessary here.

"Your brother is just worried about you," Carmine tried to placate me when I expressed my displeasure at the stationing of four guards at my own rooms in my own home. She had a sweet soul, but her deceptively small body was strong and fast. She fought best with her own hands and knew just where to hit a man to bring him down.

"We're worried too," Rufina added in her soft voice. I'd recruited her in Nishimi on my first trip several years ago. She was taller and broader and rarely spoke. She looked intimidating with her dyed bright-red hair and dark eyes, but she had such a sweet tooth that when I looked at her I didn't see the fierce warrior—I saw the woman who hoarded sweets and once knocked a man unconscious with the very bag of sugar he was trying to steal from her in the market.

"Worried for nothing. It was an unfortunate accident and he's overreacting." I crossed my arms over my chest, wincing at the way my side protested movement.

"You know the prince doesn't believe in such a thing as overreaction," Carmine teased. "But don't worry, we'll make the best of it. He said something about a tea party?"

I waved at the invitations I'd finished the day before that still waited on my writing desk. "Yes, and I need to have those delivered, as well as the menu down to the kitchens, but the party isn't until tomorrow."

"Anything else you need us to do?" Carmine asked.

"Well, I wanted to speak to the servants to hear what they knew of that girl, but as much as I hate to admit it, I don't think I'm up to it yet. My ribs hurt."

"And they'll continue to hurt for a while yet," Rufina said.

I shook my head sadly. "Lucky they're just bruised and not broken. Otherwise I suspect I'd be tied to the bed for weeks until they healed."

Both guards grinned but respected Aiden too much to voice their agreement.

Sibling privileges.

"Well," Carmine said, "we can speak to whomever you'd like for you."

"I don't know who to speak to quite yet. Just keep an ear open for now, I suppose. "

"Of course."

"But I do want to dine in court tonight. I know Aiden won't like it, but all I need to do is walk from one side of the room to the other. It would be good for them to see me."

"You could send someone in your place, you know."

I considered it. It wouldn't be the first time; since we were so completely covered in public, it was fairly easy to use body doubles when needed. I knew for a fact that my parents used them often in place of Aiden when he would sneak away.

Carmine was close enough to my build that I'd used her before, and she was clearly willing to do so again. She'd confessed she loved dressing up in my fine clothes and jewelry.

"It wouldn't be the same," I decided. "I need to see their reactions to know how to treat them. The situation is becoming too delicate for me to be ignorant of their actions."

"I understand. But if that's your plan, I'd suggest spending the afternoon resting here."

With only minor protests, she convinced me to get back into bed and relax while she entertained me with stories of her family. She had four younger sisters and never ran out of material for stories.

Sometime during the one about the time the youngest decided to help make dinner and made everyone mud pies, I drifted off to sleep.

I didn't dream, and it felt like only a moment later I heard Carmine's voice.

"It's time to get you dressed, princess," Carmine said with a gentle pat on my arm, waking me. I blinked, wiping the sleep from eyes, and rose from bed, letting her steer me to my dressing room.

"Princess," a voice called from my doorway. "I apologize for interrupting."

It was Vanna.

"No apology necessary," I said, my voice a bit thick with sleep as I redirected my course to my sitting room. I cleared my throat. "I've been hoping our paths would cross soon, but it seems you've been keeping my brother busy."

Her dark eyes were solemn behind her purple mask. She'd always been very formal and took her duties as Speaker seriously. I wondered what Aiden was doing with her, now that he spoke for himself. She was too intelligent to be a simple messenger. "I see the prince barely more than I see you," she said. "A lot of people need his attention, and I am low on the list."

"Wherever you may be on any list, I'm sure he misses your company," I assured her.

"You flatter me, princess. But I only have a moment. I wanted to express my hope that you recover from your injury quickly, and your parents from their illness as well."

"Thank you, Vanna. I appreciate your concern."

Her smile was barely noticeable, but it was there. For as often as she spoke for my family, she never spoke for herself, and I couldn't remember the last time she expressed any of her own emotions around me. I watched with curiosity as she curtseyed and let herself out.

Carmine touched my arm again. "We really need to get to work now." She had such a sooth-ing touch that I nearly drifted back to sleep as she applied powder to my face and kohl and color to my eyes. She worked quickly, moving on to my hair and humming to herself, and soon I was ready for the finishing touches.

Last came the two ivory combs I wore nearly every time I was in white. They were sturdy enough to handle my thick curls and were decorated with tiny little wildflowers on the handle.

I'd lost track of the number of times Carmine dressed my hair, so it startled me to feel the sharp prick of a comb's teeth against my scalp.

"Sorry! Did I get you?"

I frowned. The comb shouldn't be sharp enough to hurt.

"Let me see that." I held my hand out, and Carmine carefully placed the offending comb in it.

The teeth were sharp as fangs, and a single drop of blood fell into my open palm. The comb had bitten me.

"Someone sharpened this. Let me see the other one."

Carmine quickly complied. The other comb had been sharpened as well.

"Who could have done this? I wore them only a day ago, and they hadn't been tampered with then."

"We've been with you all day. Last night, perhaps?"

"Guards have been at my doors night and day. No one could have gotten in without them seeing."

My head began to pound. I dismissed it until I realized my heart was racing and my vision was going dark.

"Princess, your eyes are huge. Are you okay?" Carmine sounded panicked and I began to sway, fighting the insistent pull of unconsciousness.

More poison?

The last thing I remembered was thinking, Maybe Aiden was right after all, before collapsing in Carmine's arms.

Chapter Six

$\mathcal{M}$y throat burned with thirst as I blinked awake.

"Bianca," Aiden sighed.

"Don't," I croaked, already knowing what he was going to say.

He shook his head and handed me a glass of water, which I greedily drank.

"Do you believe someone is trying to hurt you now?"

I finished the glass before replying. "I thought I said 'Don't.'"

He ignored me. "Someone sharpened your combs and coated them with venom in hopes you'd cut yourself and it would get into your blood."

"I'm still alive, Aiden."

He was so tense he was nearly shaking with the effort to keep his emotions in check. "Barely. You don't know how close it was. If Doc hadn't been one of your guards . . . He had to try three different antidotes before your body responded, did you know that?"

Given that I'd just woken up, I did not. It didn't seem wise to answer, though.

"And it's a lucky thing he even had the right one on him. It was a venom the physicians were studying—an antidote had only just been developed. Doc picked up a dose just to be safe."

I was silent for a moment. "So the venom was already in the palace? Do you know who did this?"

Aiden shook his head and look disgusted. "I found the servant who did the deed, but he had no motive to hurt you. According to others, he'd been well paid and felt more loyalty to coin than to you."

"Where is he now?"

"Marked and exiled, like the girl." He frowned. "A punishment that hardly seems enough."

"You can be more severe with your punishments when someone actually succeeds."

"Don't even joke," he said sharply. "You've been out for five days while the venom worked its way out."

He was terrified for me. Not even a mask could hide the dark circles under his normally bright eyes. His clothes were wrinkled and his hair a mess of black curls.

"I'll have to thank Doc," I said softly, trying to steer the discussion away from my almost-death.

"Thank him on the boat. Now that you're awake, you're leaving at first light."

"What?!" I exclaimed, wincing at the way it tore at my throat.

"It's too dangerous for you here."

"It will be just as dangerous for me anywhere I go! At least here I'll be close to you and may be able to help."

I couldn't deny now that someone wanted

to hurt me, but that didn't mean I was going to run away.

"I'm not going to act like a coward and run at the first sign of danger," I insisted even as Aiden was giving directions to Carmine and Rufina to pack my things. I hadn't even noticed them, but they offered me relieved smiles as they obeyed Aiden.

"No one is calling you a coward."

"No one is going to be calling me brave, either."

He stopped and turned to give me a hard look. "There's a difference between being brave and being a fool."

"Is there really?" I muttered under my breath, though I'm sure he still heard me.

He let out an exasperated sigh. "What do you want me to do? Sit back and watch?"

"I want you to let me help."

"Because that worked so well last time."

"Sarcasm really doesn't become a king."

"Good thing I'm just a prince regent at the moment then, isn't it?"

I had an idea. I wasn't sure if it was a good idea, or if it would even work, but it was something.

I was sure, however, that Aiden would hate it.

"What if," I started slowly, easing into the idea, "I left, but only to find someone who could help?"

"I'm listening."

"You've Marked two people already. I don't think the threat of punishment is enough to stop what is happening, and I'm sure you didn't catch the true culprit."

He frowned but didn't interrupt.

"We need to be able to predict their next move, get one step ahead of them. They don't think like we do."

He was too smart to need me to continue. "You want to talk to someone who thinks like they do, like a criminal, like a murderer. Are you insane?"

"I already have someone in mind. Someone who knows parts of the palace we don't."

It took two seconds for him to make the connection.

"No. Absolutely not. Bianca," he said, exasperated, "you cannot ask me to trust the Chameleon with your safety, with your life."

"I'm not asking you to trust him; I'm asking you to trust me."

"You're asking me to gamble with your life."

"It's either my life or someone else's," I said. "If these incidents are all connected, haven't you noticed they've all targeted people around you? Who do you think will be next?"

His face paled. "Evie."

I nodded. "I don't know what this person is trying to accomplish, but it seems they want to hurt you."

"Then why not attack me directly? Why hurt so many innocents?"

"Because that hurts you more. You're a prince with growing power that seems to be making people nervous. What makes a person feel more powerless than when watching their loved ones suffer?"

He was silent for a long time, staring at his hands.

He heaved a deep sigh before finally answering. "Very well. If that's what it will take to get you away from here, and that's what you think will help, then so be it."

Chapter Seven

"ow do you know where to find him?"
Aiden asked as we stood on the docks
watching the last of the supplies being loaded
onto the ship.

"I didn't just release him into the wild
without a second thought," I said with a raised
eyebrow. We both wore our disguised masks—
his green and mine purple—but we had a lot
of practice reading each others' expressions,
even with half of our faces covered. "I left one
of my guards with him. Do you remember

Felix? He's been sending me updates while keeping an eye on our friend."

"I thought he was out with an injury," Aiden grumbled.

"He got a few scrapes, but nothing to keep him off his feet."

"And you chose not to tell me this earlier because . . . ?"

I shrugged. "I didn't know what you would do. I wanted to wait until I knew you wouldn't be reckless."

"That's everything, highnesses," Ernesto interrupted before Aiden could respond. He was the other member of my select guard, one of the youngest and always eager to please.

"Thank you, Ernesto," I said. "I'll be aboard in a moment and we can be off." He saluted and I turned back to Aiden. "Are you sure you want to keep Evie here? She's welcome to come with us."

He shook his head. "I asked her, and she said she'd prefer to stay here. I don't know what would be worse—to have her here and in danger, or with you and not knowing if she's any safer. So she'll stay close for now."

"I understand. Well, that's everything then?"

He pulled me into a tight hug and kissed the top of my head like he did every time I went away. It was never easy to leave, even knowing I had such an important mission ahead of me. I'd only barely returned.

"Don't burn anything down while I'm gone," I teased, my cheek still squished against his chest.

"That was one time," he groaned and released me.

"We'll be back in a few weeks, maybe a month. I'll send word once we know."

"I want regular updates so I know you're not dead."

"I'll do my best."

We were both stalling, but we couldn't stall forever. I could hear my guards calling to each other, readying the ship. All that was left was for me to board.

"Until we meet again." I gave his shoulder one more squeeze, turning away.

"Be careful."

Rufina was waiting for me on board and

quietly guided me to my room. It was small but clean, and I knew it was the finest available. Even though I wore the purple mask of the noble class when I traveled, my guards took care to treat me as a princess whenever possible.

"Is there anything you need?" Rufina asked from her position in my doorway.

"No, thank you." I smiled at her.

She hesitated before leaving me, though, and my smile slipped from my face. "Is something wrong?" I asked her.

She still hesitated, then stepped back in the room, closing the door behind her. "Are you sure you're making the right decision?"

"Rufina," I started, but she continued as if the floodgates had fallen open.

"Forgive me, princess, but I was with you when we caught the Chameleon on Nishima. He hurt two of your men—two of my brothers-in-arms. He fought you and would have hurt you if given the chance. Not to mention what he did in Venesia before he fled. He's killed. He killed the father of your brother's intended in order to steal his mask and identity, and then he tried to frame poor Evie for it. He tried to kill your brother—the prince himself! And I don't doubt he'd kill again if cornered. Should we really be hunting him down again? And to ask for his help?"

"I don't need to be reminded of what he's done," I said softly, reaching for her hands and holding them in my own. It was rare to see her so worked up. "But I disagree with you on one point—I don't think he would kill again, not if he had any other choice. He was desperate, and alone, and a cruel person took advantage of him. I watched him see the girl he loved die in front of him. He's not the Chameleon anymore, not really. His name is Joch."

She pressed her lips together in a thin line.

"And as I've told Aiden, he saved my life. He could have killed me when we fought to capture him."

"Not killing you is not the same as saving your life."

I sighed. "Sparing it, then. But surely you could see why I wouldn't say that to my brother."

"You like him," she accused gently.

"What? No, of course not!" I dropped her hands and backed away. "I respect him and want to help him."

Her dark eyes were shrewd, and I could see she didn't believe me.

"I'm not foolish enough to deny that, yes, he is attractive, but I'm also not foolish enough to think that anything could ever happen between us. Aside from Aiden despising him, he is likely still mourning the loss of that girl."

Rufina just looked at me. I hated how she could make me talk without saying a thing.

"If anything, it's just a passing fancy." I needed to stop talking. "I admire a good fighter and someone who goes after what they want. That's all."

"If you insist, princess. I'll be just outside your door if you need anything." She nodded and left with a blank expression on her face, made even more difficult to read with the black half-mask she wore.

I glared at the closed door.

Even more than my traitorous mouth, I hated the way my right hand tingled with the faint memory of a farewell kiss.

Chapter Eight

The journey passed uneventfully, and I spent much of it anxiously resting, urging my ribs to heal more quickly. When we finally sighted the shoreline of Nishima, I couldn't wait to get my feet on solid ground and get to work.

My first task was to find Felix, the guard I'd left to keep track of Joch's whereabouts. I took Ernesto with me while the others secured our rooms at a local inn. Venesians were usually fairly easy to spot abroad. No one else

wore the masks we did, and very few Venesians were comfortable removing their masks
in public, even if no one else was wearing one.
With any mask, Felix would stand out here,
but with a guard's black mask, he would be
impossible to miss.

"You know I could handle this part on my
own," Ernesto said as we walked down the
street.

"Yes, but I'm impatient. And I have a good
feeling about finding Felix quickly, especially
if what he's written about Joch is true."

"Oh?"

"He's gotten a job working here and didn't
seem to be leaving anytime soon. With any
luck, he should still be here."

"Here? In a port town? Isn't that a little
risky? Especially with a black-masked guard
around?"

I agreed, but I couldn't pretend to understand Joch's motives for what he did. "Perhaps,
but it's a risk that I'm grateful he took. The
faster we can return home, the happier I'll be."

The first stop was the shipping office
through which Felix sent us his messages.

As planned, Felix left word with the captain about his whereabouts in case we needed to reach him, and from there it was only a matter of a short trip to the other side of town before we found him.

And then, before I knew it, he was directing me to where Joch was.

I wasn't expecting to see him so soon. I'd had a week of sea travel to prepare, but somehow that hadn't been enough time. He was here, and he might be the key to saving my family and my country.

I stepped inside the small stable, the warm scent of hay and animals washing over me. There were three stalls and I could hear someone moving around in the furthest one, speaking in low tones to the horse he tended.

I approached and recognized him before he even turned around.

"Joch," I said in a soft voice so as not to spook the horses—or the young man.

He started and then turned to face me. It seemed the instant recognition was mutual. He looked me up and down, his gaze lingering on my noble's mask.

I'm not sure what I expected him to do, but I expected him to do something. Instead, he turned back to the horse he was grooming and resumed brushing the warm brown coat.

"You remember me?" I prompted him, not sure what to say at his lack of reaction.

He chuckled, a sad, soft sound, and the horse nickered in return.

"You're difficult to forget," he replied.

I opened my mouth to respond and then closed it again, shifting my weight from foot to foot. Then I said, "You don't seem surprised to see me."

He shrugged. "I knew it was only a matter of time before our paths crossed again."

"You don't seem very concerned about my being here."

He finally put the brush away and approached me, draping his long arms across the stall door. Light streamed in from the stable windows, highlighting the scarred Mark on his cheek—a chameleon's curled tail with slash through it. My breath caught in my throat to see it.

I thought I'd grown immune to the shock

of seeing bare faces, but apparently not when it came to his.

"You're alone, and it's the middle of the day. You would've needed to speak to the stable owners to know where I was, so they'd know a noble Venesian lady was here, and if anything happened to me, such a bold attack would reflect badly on your country. Not to mention the fact that I'm in a stable, surrounded by any number of tools I could easily turn to weapons."

"I'm not alone," I argued, feeling foolish.

He looked pointedly around us, where we were surrounded by no one but horses and a curious brown barn cat perched on a stall door.

"I didn't come here unaccompanied," I clarified. "But I thought it best to approach you by myself. I didn't want to scare you."

He laughed again, this time with more feeling behind it. "I'm sorry to be the one to tell you this, but you're not very intimidating, little princess."

I drew my shoulders back sharply. It was true that he was a full head taller than me, but I had power and influence that most found very intimidating indeed. I changed tactics. "I could be here to arrest you again. Even the people here know what our Marks mean, and you're not exactly trying to hide yours."

"I grew tired of hiding. And the horses hardly care."

I sighed. "So you're not even going to try to run from me?"

He read the confusion on my face. "Why would I bother running? You clearly have an informant on me or you wouldn't have been able to find me so quickly, so I doubt there's somewhere I could easily hide. And if you wanted to kill me, you wouldn't have set me free in the first place."

"Maybe I changed my mind," I said, not liking how easily he surrendered. Where was the boy as I'd last seen him, the one who fought tooth and nail to survive?

"You don't strike me as fickle, princess." He raised an eyebrow.

He made me nervous. But I needed him.

"I have a proposal for you."

Chapter Nine

proposal?"

I nodded.

He sighed. "So it's time to pay for my freedom?"

"Venesia is in trouble," I said, avoiding his question. "Someone is attacking the royal family, and the court is growing nervous. They don't trust my brother and he is too distracted to care what they think. I'm worried if something isn't done soon, we'll have a coup on our hands."

"Attacking the royal family?"

"Poison seems to be the weapon of choice. Both my parents are on bed rest and I was attacked twice before Aiden sent me away."

"You've been attacked?" That seemed to get his attention, but it wasn't enough for him to drop his defenses. "Why would you need me?"

"We need to be able to anticipate this attacker's moves, something you'd be much better at than we ever could be. You think in a certain way. And I suspect you know things about the palace that even I don't. You would make an excellent guard."

He gave me a long look. "And if I say no? Would you take me back by force?"

I hadn't even considered the possibility of him rejecting my offer. "Why would you refuse?'

"Why should I accept? Nothing good has happened to me in Venesia. I have no desire to return. I'm a wanted murdered and traitor there." He raised an eyebrow at me.

I pursed my lips and then said, "I'm offering you a chance to become more than that, a chance to redeem yourself."

"What's the point? I'm not Venesian and never have been. I don't care what they think of me."

"Don't you care about making things right?"

"I made the mistake of caring before. I don't care about much of anything anymore." He straightened and exited the stall, making as if to carry on with his work in an attempt to dismiss me.

I wasn't so easily dismissed.

"I didn't free you so you could throw the rest of your life away hiding in a tiny town fit for no company but the horses you tend to. You have talents and you used to have drive," I said to his back as he walked away. "Don't tell me I was wrong to hope for more for you."

He stopped. Without turning around, he said in a detached voice, "What do you want from me?"

Frustration made me antsy, made me reckless. "I want you to show some signs of life. To care about something. Fight me."

"Fight you?" He laughed once, softly, and then seemed to consider my request. "If I win, will you leave me alone?"

No. "Perhaps."

He turned around. "Then if that's what it will take . . ." He lunged toward me.

We'd fought one-on-one once before, and I'd seen him fight others more than once. Two small daggers were his weapons of choice, and they had always been hidden in sheaths on his legs and drawn in the blink of an eye. I expected them, and even though I wore no weapon to counter him, I was quick and wore guards on my forearms that could be used to shield me.

He didn't draw them on me.

Instead he came at me with his fists empty and relaxed. He grabbed for my wrists, but I was faster and twisted out of reach.

"I said a fight, not a game of catch-me-if-you-can." I scowled at him.

"You're unarmed and I'm not going to punch you."

"I didn't plan on letting you."

"No one plans to get punched."

I laughed in spite of myself. "You've seen me fight before. You know I can defend myself. Have you lost your touch? Grown soft already?"

He scowled back at me. "If I give you a black eye, nothing you could do would stop your brother from killing me the instant I set foot in Venesia, deal or not."

True, but irrelevant. "Would you rather leave your fate to a flip of a coin or a game of cards?" I asked, growing exasperated when he made no move to attack again.

"Fate's as good a judge as any of what I'll do with my life."

"Your life is too important to leave to chance! Do something!" I flew at him, my patience overruled by frustration.

My right fist made contact with his cheek.

He reeled back, blinking, and lifted one hand to touch the skin that doubtless would soon be sporting a bruise.

I didn't give him any more time to react, pulling my left fist back to strike again. He blocked me this time, his eyes narrowing. I didn't hesitate, drawing upon years of hand-to-hand combat training. He only blocked, and my punches weren't forceful enough to break through his defenses. I would tire before he did if he kept up that method, but I had little choice in the matter.

"Do you not even care enough about yourself to fight?" I taunted him, my blood pumping.

"You're on a fool's errand," he responded after a moment. "As I said, I don't care about anything."

He turned away from me again and sprinted for the exit.

My hands falling to my sides, my breathing heavy, I watched him run away. I wasn't going to give up so easily—even if he wanted to.

Chapter Ten

When Joch was in hiding in Venesia as the Chameleon, he worked as a glass blower, and he'd been quite talented. Quiet, but undeniably skilled. That kind of talent didn't just happen. He must have had some kind of training before the tragedy that turned him into the Chameleon had happened. I didn't know all the details, but I knew it involved the death of a girl very close to him. And I'd watched helplessly as he'd lost someone again. I doubted either would be happy with what he was now.

But that was about the sum of all I knew of him. I needed more.

The next morning I met with Felix again. "What did you learn about him while he's been here?" I asked as we sat down to breakfast at the inn.

"Not much, I'm afraid. He keeps to himself and doesn't really leave the stables even when he has free time."

I thought for a moment. "Does he have any family? Has he been in contact with anyone at all?"

Felix shook his head. "Not that I know of. He hasn't sent or received any messages. He just works and broods."

I shot him a look. He shrugged.

"That's the best word for it. He just sits in the loft above the stables and stares out the window for hours. He sleeps a lot. He doesn't talk to anyone except the family he's working for, and even then it's only about the animals."

I chewed on my bottom lip, thinking.

"He seems to like that cat, though. The ugly barn cat? It keeps finding its way up the tree just outside the stable, and he's rescued it every time. He pretends to ignore it, but he doesn't, not the way it meows and follows him around like a kitten after its mama."

An amusing picture, but not a particularly helpful piece of information for what I was after. I had no one to question, no one with any clue to his past. All I had was Joch himself.

Resigned, I returned to the stables where I found him mucking out the stalls. The horses were out of sight and the stable was eerily quiet without them.

"Need a hand?" I asked, peering at him over the wooden divider.

He didn't jump at the sound of my voice, just scoffed at my offer. "A princess mucking stalls? Do you even know how?"

"I wasn't allowed to take riding lessons until I did," I informed him smartly. Granted, it had been years since I had last touched a pitchfork, but my back had faced the aching work that was shoveling hay and manure.

"Of course not," he muttered, and I

suspected he hadn't meant for me to hear so I didn't respond. Instead, I held out a hand.

"Just tell me what needs to be done and I'll do it."

We worked in silence for a long time. I could feel blisters forming on my hands, but I wasn't going to complain. I was making progress just by being here.

So I didn't leave.

I accompanied him on all his chores, from mucking the stalls to cleaning the mud off the horses' coats. To my amusement, I noticed that mangy cat following us as well, watching me with a suspicious glare, as if it knew I was there to take Joch away. I'd tried to pet it, but it only hissed and swiveled its ears back. That was fine. I didn't need to win over the cat as well, only the young man.

Joch rarely let me do anything, so I just watched and waited patiently with a small smile on my lips, knowing it was only a matter of time before I wore him down.

And I did it again the next day, and the day after that.

On the third day, we were walking the

length of the pasture checking for damage in the fence when my patience was rewarded.

"You're not going to leave until I come with you, are you?" he asked, breaking the silence between us.

"I'm not afraid to fight for what I want. And if biding my time is what it takes, then so be it."

He sighed. "What's really stopping you from taking me back to Venesia by force?"

"A reluctant guard is worse than no guard at all," I scoffed.

He paused. Then said, "Explain."

"A guard who doesn't want to be there can be bribed," I said patiently. "Or careless. Or a distraction. Or any number of unhelpful things."

He was silent for a long time. "I need proof. I have no reason to trust you."

"I set you free. And I've left you alone since then. You need more proof than that?"

"You left a spy with me. I was never alone."

"But I did set you free."

His dark eyes bored into mine. "And I don't understand why. So, yes, I still need proof."

His words left me strangely warm and unbalanced. I wasn't used to having to prove myself—I was a princess of Venesia. An ambassador whose word was good as gold.

But none of that meant anything to Joch, the former Chameleon, an assassin, alone in the world.

How could I prove anything to him?

Chapter Eleven

Instead of going straight to the stable in the morning as I usually did, I went for a long walk, mulling over my problem. When I was no closer to a solution at noon than I had been at sunrise, I reluctantly turned to the stables, hoping inspiration would strike as I worked more with Joch.

It felt oddly quiet as I approached, and instantly I knew something was wrong. I couldn't see what it was; this time of day, the horses were all either in the pasture or being used for labor or transport.

Then I smelled smoke.

I rushed into the stable where Joch was undoubtedly working or eating inside, away from the hot sun.

I ran from stall to stall, looking for either flames or Joch and finding neither—until I reached the furthest stall. Normally it didn't even house an animal and was used to store hay and a handful of tools.

Hay that burned and burned quickly.

In the seconds I took in the sight before me, flames engulfed a bale and jumped to another. Shouting for Joch, I dashed to the water barrel. "Joch, where are you? Joch!"

I stopped in my tracks when I reached the barrel. It had been tipped over, and now the only water left was in the muddy ground.

The fire was no accident. Someone wanted this stable to burn.

I needed to find Joch.

I ignored the sinking feeling in my stomach and the whisper of a thought suggesting if he was behind this, if he was so desperate to be left alone that he would burn the place down to escape me.

"What's wrong?"

I spun around, and there he was. When I saw his face, I instantly regretted my suspicion. He looked worried, his eyes scanning me from head to toe. "Is something wrong? Are you hurt?" Then he noticed the overturned barrel. "What happened to the water barrel?"

There was no time to explain my suspicions. "There's a fire in the stable. Quick, in the unused stall!"

His face paled and he ran toward the flames with me on his heels. He skidded to a stop once the fire was in sight and I nearly ran into him.

"Are the animals all out?"

"I think so," I said. "None of the horses were inside. I didn't see the cat."

"She's smart. She'll have gotten herself out," he muttered, more to himself than to me. "That's good but we still need to save the building."

"But there's no more water," I said quickly.

His eyes darted back and forth as he thought. Then he instructed me, "Grab the blankets. We'll smother it as best we can."

"That won't be enough."

"We have to do something," he insisted.

But the fire had already spread to the support posts. "I don't think we can stop it. The best we can do is do get as much out of there as we can. Save supplies."

He let out a frustrated shout. "Fine. You carry as much of the food and grain out as you can, and I'll see what I can save from this end before the fire gets to it."

He had a wild look in his eyes. I didn't want to leave him, but there wasn't time to argue and the stable was small enough that I wouldn't be far.

Sweat dripped down my neck and back as I hauled feed bags outside, and for the first time I regretted not bringing my guards with me. We needed more hands.

The wood began to crack as the fire gained power and the air was filled with the scent of smoke and ash.

"Joch, it's time! We need to get out!" I couldn't see him through the flames and smoke, and shouted his name over and over again.

The path to the tack room where I'd last seen him was blocked. He could be trapped inside.

My heart raced and I sprinted around the outside of the stable to try to enter from the other side.

"Princess!" I spun around at the sound and saw Carmine and Rufina racing toward me. "We smelled fire. Are you hurt?"

"I think Joch is still inside!" I said, turning back to the stable.

"What happened?"

"I don't know—I don't have time to explain. I have to find him." I saw them exchange concerned looks.

"Princess, please." Rufina gripped my upper arms and spoke in a low voice. "Tell us what you need us to do."

"I need you to help me find him!"

A loud crash came from the tack room.

I didn't think. I just ran.

I shook free of Rufina's grasp and ran through the flames, my eyes stinging from the smoke. I pulled the front of my dress up over my nose and mouth, and pushed myself through the smoke toward the tack room. I saw Joch's figure standing in the middle of the room, a wall of flame in the doorway. His eyes were wide and blank and unseeing, not even noticing me as I shouted his name.

I had no choice. I gathered my clothes close around me and jumped through the doorway. I grabbed Joch, shaking him hard as I shouted over the dull roar of the stable burning down around us.

"Joch! We need to go! Joch, can you hear me?" My throat was dry and I could barely find my voice.

He blinked rapidly, turning ever so slightly to look at me.

I pulled on his arm, yanking him toward the exit.

He took a step but still seemed too far away. I took his hand in mine and shouted in his ear, my voice raspy, "Just follow me, okay? I've got you."

Obedient as a child, his fingers curled around mine. I flinched as a support beam collapsed outside the room. We didn't have much time, and if I didn't act quickly we'd both be trapped.

"Now run!" I shouted, pulling him behind me. We cleared the doorway and I didn't stop running until Carmine caught hold of me outside. She quickly smothered the tiny flames that had latched onto my skirt, her hands wrapped in strips torn from her own clothing. Joch collapsed to the ground beside me, coughing violently.

I heard more voices approach as the fire spread to the roof.

"Rufina went for more help," Carmine explained in her soft, reassuring voice. "You're done now, princess. You can rest now. There's nothing more you can do."

I fell to my knees.

Soot clung to my eyelashes as I watched men from the village move what supplies we'd already rescued further away. There was nothing that could be done for the structure anymore.

"Stay here," Carmine instructed. "I'm going to find you water and then we'll go back to the inn so you can rest."

I nodded to show I understood, and then Joch and I were alone, save for the cat that had appeared out of nowhere and had stretched protectively over his feet. Joch scratched her behind the ears but barely seemed to notice he was even doing it.

I looked at him. There was still a slightly glazed look to his eyes, but he seemed to have shaken himself from whatever spell he was under and was watching the men work.

"You came after me," he said in a low, husky voice, not looking at me.

"I did."

"Why would you do that?"

"I had to. You might have died."

He paused. "Would that have been such a bad thing?"

I gasped and reached for his face, forcing him to look at me.

"Yes, Joch, that would have been a bad thing. I know your life isn't going the way you expected and I know you're still mourning a great loss, but that's no reason to just give up now."

His eyes stared into mine, filled with too many emotions to name. Fear? Shame? I pulled my hand back but he didn't look away.

"I froze in there," he said. "Do you know why?"

I shook my head.

"That's not the first time I've been surrounded by flames. The last time, I had just killed a man for his mask. I mocked and Marked his daughter. At the time, I thought I was doing the right thing. I thought I was doing it to save the one I loved. But I was wrong. And it all came back to me just now."

I didn't know what to say.

"So you see why I have a hard time caring about anything. It hurts too much."

"Well," I said, not looking away. "If you're not going to care about yourself, then I'll just do it for you."

"What?"

"I don't know how better to explain it to you than reminding you that I just ran into a burning stable for you. I didn't have to stop and think about it—I just did. The same way I would have for any one of my guards or friends or family. I care about everyone. I can care about you too."

He didn't say anything for a long time,

just looked at me with that odd expression I couldn't read. Eventually, he sighed and turned back to watch the stable.

"You win. I'll go with you back to Venesia."

Chapter Twelve

"Your guards are entirely too cheerful," Joch observed that evening as we made arrangements to return home. I'd instructed Felix to stay behind to help with the aftermath of the fire, and in case whoever started it came back for more trouble. He'd happily agreed and left to inform Joch's former boss of the plan.

"I like to surround myself with happy people. I find it makes life a lot easier."

"And yet you were determined to drag me

into your life. I think you'll find I complicate it somewhat."

"I said easier, not easy. I'm not afraid of complications."

"That's been well established."

I rolled my eyes and reached for a fresh piece of parchment. I wanted to leave written instructions with a royal seal, so Felix could have access to whatever funds he needed. I suspected our presence was to blame for the fire, and I wanted to help make amends for the owner's loss. Plus, I was taking away his primary hired hand.

"We'll leave in the morning," I informed Joch as I wrote. "The weather is good now and we'll want to get ahead of any summer storms that might spring up. And I'm anxious to return as soon as possible."

"Have you had word of any more attacks or suspicious behavior?"

I pulled Aiden's letter out of my writing desk and offered it to him. "My brother suspects everyone, but nothing new has happened while I've been away."

Joch scanned the letter quickly, his

expression twisting into a wry smile. "He's not exactly looking forward to my being around you, is he?"

That was putting it lightly. Aiden had reached the point of trying to bribe me to abandon this plan, but there was nothing I wanted badly enough to agree, and nothing that I couldn't simply get myself.

I shrugged. "He'll come around. This is too important for him to sulk about for too long."

"He has good reason."

I ignored him. "You'll want to say any good-byes tonight. We'll leave very early in the morning."

"I don't have anyone that will miss me."

His words pricked something inside me and I wanted to instantly protest and tell him that wasn't true. He seemed to know it too and met my eyes with a challenge in his own. But I didn't know his life here, and if what Felix had told me was true, it was possible no one would miss him.

Except maybe one. "What about the barn cat? She seemed to be attached to you. Did you want to take her with us? Cats can be useful on ships."

He grew flustered for a moment and turned away. "She's not mine to take. She doesn't even have a name."

"She doesn't need a name to have feelings."

"She's a cat."

"It doesn't matter. Don't forget to bid her farewell," I said. "Because I think she'll miss you, even if you think no one else will."

He didn't deny it. And later that night when he was supposed to be in a room shared with one of my guards but was suspiciously absent, I wasn't worried. I knew he didn't forget.

The next morning was a blur as we started the long trip back to Venesia. Joch, as it turned out, was not much of a sailor and tended to get in the way more than he helped, and he eventually gave up, retreating to the bunk he would share with the other male guards. There wasn't much for me to do, so after a quick stop in my own bunk to fetch something, I followed him.

After a brief knock on the door, I pushed it open. "May I come in?" I asked.

There were three hammocks strung from the ceiling in the small space, and he was sitting in one of them, his feet firmly on the ground. "I suppose."

"I have something for you," I said, holding out the mask I'd brought from my bunk.

He sighed heavily. "I suppose it's unavoidable. Venesians and their masks . . . a person might as well not have a face without one."

"You dislike them that much?"

"They hide too many secrets."

"Sometimes it's best for secrets to remain hidden," I said gently, unable to keep my eyes from flickering to the scarred Mark on his cheek. "Sometimes people can't handle them."

He made a noncommittal humming sound and took the mask from my hands. "Blue?"

I nodded. "I thought it simplest since blue is the most common. Wear purple like the nobles and you'd be instantly discovered. Black like my guards and you'd raise suspicion. Blue is for those work with the sea, and they're rarely seen as threatening by anyone in the palace."

He turned the mask over in his hands, examining it. It was a pale blue, the lighter shade a symbol of prosperity and success, with waves of silver and sea green, more symbols of the sea. With this mask, people would assume he was a high-ranking commoner, likely a sea trader, and shouldn't question his presence in the palace. Most nobles wouldn't bother to talk to him, but at least he'd be able to walk around without causing problems. Most of the time he would be with me anyway.

"Thank you." He reluctantly put it on, and I was surprised to realize I was sad to see his face disappear. I'd grown used to it as one of the few unmasked faces I saw regularly. My guards were always masked, as was I. With the exception of Rufina, all of us were too deeply Venesian and felt too exposed without the masks.

"I might as well start getting used to it again," he continued.

I nodded. "I'll want to get to work as soon

as we arrive. We'll catch up with Aiden to learn of any new developments and go from there."

"And what is it exactly that I'll be doing?"

"I'm not exactly sure yet," I confessed. "First I want to make sure you're familiar with the situation and the palace."

"Oh, I'm very familiar with the palace. I may even know more about it than you do."

I narrowed my eyes at him. "What makes you say that?"

"I know the royal family has secret tunnels and rooms and exits, but so do the servants. Or they did, a long time ago, and they're rarely used now. Most probably don't know they exist."

I knew of them, but I thought they'd been collapsed or bricked in. I didn't know where they were or that they were even still usable. "Why do you know this?"

"I was taught about them by the man who wanted me to kill your brother."

I knew his history but it was still jarring to hear the words.

"They're tricky to navigate but they're still

there," he continued, carefully watching my expression. "And if I know about them, there's always the possibility that someone else might too."

"I know," I said, my voice grim. "That's why you're going to show them to me."

Chapter Thirteen

*A*iden was waiting for us at the docks, as I knew he would be.

He stood with his back straight, alone, and wearing the green mask he favored when sneaking out of the palace. I'd seen him in so many different masks that I would have recognized him no matter what he wore. But it was nice to see one so familiar.

Joch came to stand beside me, leaning against the wooden railing with his back to the shore and crossing his arms. The closer we'd gotten to Venesia, the more tense and still he'd become. Whereas Aiden paced when he was anxious or upset, Joch seemed to be the opposite and grew incredibly still. More than once I'd walked above deck and not noticed him until he acknowledged my presence.

"Is he out here?" he asked.

I nodded. "Alone, though, if that eases your conscious at all."

He scoffed. "I still feel like a mouse walking into a trap."

"A very tall mouse."

He blinked at me.

I offered him a small smile. "Just trying to lighten the mood somewhat."

He grunted. I could tell I needed to try something new.

"I could tell you embarrassing stories about Aiden as a child. Would that help calm you down?"

"I don't need to be calmed down."

A bald-faced lie if I ever heard one. He stood as still as a statue, and as rigid and cold as one as well.

"He used to sneak out of the palace all the

time. He did it so frequently that my parents assigned a young guard to be his double, so when he went missing, no one else would know. But, oh, how he'd be punished when he finally came home."

Joch didn't say anything, but I could tell his interest was piqued. I waited patiently with a smile until he finally gave in and asked, "What kind of punishments?"

"They never really found one that was effective, though it wasn't for lack of trying. First they tried confining him to his room, but that was pointless; he knew exactly how to escape. They tried giving him more lessons and responsibilities so that he'd be too busy, but that only gave him more things to run away from. They tried taking away sweets, then giving him extra if he promised to behave. They tried guilting him, shaming him, bribing him. None of it worked. To him, nothing was worth staying inside."

"He's stubborn."

I laughed. "You don't know the half of it. If he gets it in his mind to do something, there's no stopping him. He had a tutor who said he was too impatient to memorize our history, so he memorized the royal family line back as far as we know out of spite. He used to be awful at fencing, but he was determined to be the best and practiced relentlessly. Now there are few that can match him." I shrugged. "But he's also nearly drowned more than once by thinking he's a stronger swimmer than he actually is. And few people will bother to argue with him because it can be so exhausting, so he's gotten used to getting his way or assuming he's right. He's lucky he still has me to set him straight when the situation calls for it."

"You love him a lot," Joch observed quietly. I couldn't read his expression.

I glanced at him and couldn't help but smile. "I do. He's my brother."

A much less tense silence fell between us, though it was still not exactly relaxed.

"Give me a moment before you come out," I warned Joch. "I should . . . warm him up a little."

"Probably a good idea," he said dryly.

Aiden's eyes darted from mine to the ship as I disembarked, waiting.

"Good to see you too, brother," I greeted him.

"Did you find him?"

"Yes."

"And?"

"He's agreed to help."

"Where is he?"

"On the ship. I didn't want to spring you two on each other." I surveyed the crowd, amazed when I didn't see any of his guards hidden among the people hurrying past. "Honestly, I'm surprised you showed such restraint. I was half expecting a royal procession."

"I was tempted, believe me. Would have given that piece of scum a nice surprise."

I shot him a hard look.

"But I decided stealth was the better option. Court never knew you left, thanks to your double. And I certainly didn't want to draw attention to the Chameleon returning."

I nodded. "For the best, I think. Very well. Are you ready to meet him?"

"As ready as I'll ever be."

I turned and raised my hand, giving Joch the all-clear.

I don't know exactly what I'd expected—maybe some deference or unease in his posture, some outward sign of nervousness or discomfort. But, no, Joch strode down the plank with his shoulders back and chin up, looking as dangerous as I'd ever seen him. His face was carefully blank behind the pale blue mask I'd provided for him.

He stepped onto the pier and faced Aiden.

"So," Aiden said, his voice hard and cold. "It's you."

"As you see." Joch smirked.

I winced inwardly as Aiden frowned, looking him up and down. I'd hoped they'd get off to a better start than this. Instead, my brother calmly shifted his weight, drew back his right arm, and punched Joch square in the face.

Chapter Fourteen

$\mathcal{D}$id you have to antagonize him?" I asked Joch as I pressed a cooling salve to his bare cheekbone. It still sent a bit of a thrill through me to be so close to his bare face, but I traveled so often that naked faces didn't scandalize me the way they might have other members of the court, and I didn't want to call for any of the court physicians.

"I don't want him thinking me weak," he replied simply.

"He wasn't thinking that." I was quick to defend my brother.

Joch raised a thick eyebrow.

"He wasn't," I insisted. "If he thought you were weak, he wouldn't be so worried for my safety when I'm with you."

"And yet we're alone now."

"It's the middle of the day, and we're in the middle of the palace," I said. "He knows you're not stupid." I knew Aiden was afraid of Joch, but it felt disloyal to mention that. "What would hurting me now accomplish?"

Staring at me, he murmured, "What indeed?"

My eyes flickered to the Mark on his quickly swelling cheek. It was the source of his nickname—a scroll of a chameleon's tail with a slash through it. I wondered briefly what he'd first done to earn it. Venesian Marks were not handed out lightly, and he'd been branded before he began his mission to assassinate the prince.

He noticed my distraction.

"My master gave it to me," he said. "As a reminder of who I needed to be in order to get what I wanted. He told me to think of her when he branded me, and whenever I felt discouraged, to look at it to remind myself of what I was working towards."

His eyes met mine and I couldn't bring myself to look away. There was so much to him that I didn't know, that I didn't understand. I only knew who he meant by "her"—his childhood sweetheart who'd been used to trick him into becoming an assassin, who'd been his whole reason for being until she died in his arms.

Would I ever feel that kind of devotion to someone outside my family?

"We should get going," I said suddenly, shoving his mask toward him and looking away. "My brother wants to meet with you to discuss our arrangement."

Aiden wanted us to meet him in the throne room, presumably in an attempt to further intimidate Joch, though I could see no outward signs of nerves. His expression was blank as Aiden greeted me and remained blank as Aiden began to speak.

Aiden didn't apologize for his behavior earlier. He also didn't waste any time getting to the reason he and Joch were forced to bear each other's company.

"This is called loveslock," he said, holding up a small green bottle. "You will take a spoonful each morning. It is a slow-acting venom—to ensure you don't try anything . . . unsavory. I will give you the antidote each night."

"I know what it is," Joch said. He didn't elaborate how. "It will turn deadly after so many doses."

"Then you better fulfill your duty quickly."

"Aiden," I warned.

"It's a small dosage," he told me. "Too much would knock him out and leave him to die a slow, unconscious death, and—while I would be happier—he'd be useless."

I frowned at him but didn't say anything more.

"You will also be acting as the princess's taste-tester. You will try any food before she eats it, and any drink."

"Her attacker has yet to strike by food or drink," Joch pointed out. "Am I to touch everything she owns before she does as well?"

Aiden scowled. "You are to guard her as best you can."

"So let me make sure I understand: you want me to willingly drink poison and trust you to give me an antidote each night. Then, while I have said poison in my body, you want me to protect the princess by potentially putting more poison into my body. Meanwhile, I'm also to protect her from an unknown attacker and try to find out who's behind this whole affair?"

I hadn't stopped to think just how much we were asking of him until he laid it out so succinctly. Aiden smirked, and I wanted to pinch him.

"That sounds about right," he replied, crossing his arms and looking far too smug.

"I came here by my own choice. I'm not going to willingly drink poison to prove myself."

"You are wanted for murder and treason and you are standing before two members of the royal family with a number of guards at hand. It's either poison or prison at this point."

"Aiden," I said sharply. "I told him I didn't want to force him to obey. By weakening him, you're weakening me as well."

"A condition I'm willing to accept. I cannot and will not let him walk free without some way to keep him in check. I don't trust him, and I don't trust his motives."

"We've already been through this. I'm not asking you to trust him; I'm asking you to trust me." My temper was rising, fueled by the embarrassment of arguing with Aiden in front of Joch.

Aiden balked, and I could see him struggling to keep from saying something he'd regret: he didn't trust me, not when Joch was concerned.

But I knew he was thinking it.

We glared at each other. I knew he was stubborn, but we were siblings after all was said and done. I was equally stubborn.

"I'll do it." Joch's voice was unexpected, but firm.

"What?" Aiden and I simultaneously exclaimed and turned to him, equally shocked. Aiden's response was more tinged with irritation than confusion. He didn't want Joch to accept his stipulations. He wanted Joch in prison or, better yet, the executioner's block.

"I owe you my life. You seem to have more use for it than I ever did." His words were directed toward me, but he never took his eyes off my brother. "I'm not afraid."

Aiden didn't look particularly pleased, even though he'd gotten his way.

Tired of being in the same room with the pair of them, I sent Joch to wash up and rest after our journey and headed toward my own quarters to do the same, but Aiden followed me to my room where he impatiently paced from one side to the other.

"He's suicidal."

"He's doing what you asked of him! Is there no pleasing you?"

He grunted. "No."

"Just give him a chance," I pleaded. "Let him show you things have changed. He's changed. You have all the power here, and you both know that, so there's no need to be so pig-headed. If he betrays us, then you can gloat and send him to prison. But wouldn't you rather he try to make up for what he did? Isn't that a more productive form of punishment?"

The frown still didn't leave his face. "I still don't like it. Or him. I will never like him."

"I know. I know that would truly be impossible."

Chapter Fifteen

I was impatient to learn more about
those secret passages Joch had mentioned, but we needed to wait until night
when most of the palace was asleep. We
couldn't be seen together until he formally
arrived by dining with the court, and there
hadn't been time to prepare him tonight. It
was probably better that we both rest before
facing court anyway.

So that left me anxiously pacing my room
and picking at the tray of food that had been

brought up earlier until Carmine or Rufina could declare the way clear.

"You should really consider taking a few days to rest," Carmine said nervously, rearranging the dishes on my tray for the third time. "Or at least eat more. Here, eat another biscotto."

"I don't have time to rest," I replied, but I did take a biscotto and nibbled on it. Rufina helped herself to one as well, and rolled her eyes.

"Well," she said as she munched on the hard biscuit, "I don't think it's the best idea to be wandering around the palace with th—"

I cleared my throat, giving Rufina a pointed look. "Joch," she continued elegantly, as if she was always intending to use his proper name. "Especially alone with him."

"Too many people would attract too much attention," I reminded her.

"I still don't like it."

"Noted. Is anyone else coming to see me tonight?"

"No, anyone who might have wanted to agrees with me that you need your rest."

"Then I'm changing."

I'd hoped to have a black mask to wear tonight, but as they were only worn by guards, they were carefully accounted for. I could order one, of course, but there wasn't time and it might have raised suspicion. A silver one would have to do. I'd used a servant's silver mask plenty of times before whenever I wanted to move about the palace unnoticed. After changing into the uniform of a dark dress and smock, I was ready to go.

Joch couldn't meet me in my suite, and I couldn't visit him in the guest quarters without drawing attention to myself—he would have already had servants assigned to his room— so Carmine accompanied me to a meeting point while Rufina fetched him. Rufina had insisted on being the one to get him.

"I need to remind him of the consequences to any actions he might be inclined to take," she'd said, wrapping her hand around the hilt of the dagger sheathed at her hip.

"Behave."

"Of course, princess."

When she appeared with Joch at her heels,

they were both in one piece. He looked like he was still waking up, and I felt a little bad for not letting him rest longer, but I knew he must be as impatient as I was to get started. Or if not impatient, curious.

"All right, lead the way," I said, gesturing in front of me after I bid farewell to my guards. They reluctantly watched as Joch began leading with a startling level of surety in his path.

"You do know your way around," I murmured as we snaked through the palace.

"I have a good memory."

We finally stopped in the Hall of Portraits, a large, ornate room covered in portraits of kings and queens of Venesia, dating back to before we wore white. It was also a very public room, and I shot Joch a puzzled glance.

"Here?"

"Here." He looked over his shoulder, then reached behind the edge of the frame of a former king dressed in white. My great-grandfather. I heard a soft click, and the portrait swung open. Joch looked at me expectantly.

"But this room is open to anyone in the palace."

"Exactly. No one would look suspicious coming here."

"B-but," I sputtered, my mind racing. "How has this never been discovered before?"

"This may be a public room, but it's not a popular one. And you may be relieved to know that guards do come through here often, and, of course, touching the portraits is discouraged. Now come, we shouldn't linger."

I hoisted myself up into the opening, which was at about hip height for me. There was a small platform, then three steps back to floor level. Joch closed the portrait behind us, and we were alone in the dark.

"No lantern?" I whispered.

"Give your eyes a moment to adjust. You'll see."

I'd expected it to be pitch black, but in a moment, I was surprised by how well I could see. Light leaked in from the Hall of Portraits, giving us just enough to see by.

"Where are the holes? How is the light getting in?"

"Most are too high up for anyone in the room to see or notice, and they're so small that most people wouldn't notice them without specifically looking for them. Even if they did see them, they probably wouldn't be able to guess what they were. Lanterns are too dangerous in such close quarters and could give away a person's presence. There are holes like this all along the passageway. I'll show you."

I shivered.

The passage was only about shoulder-width long, and while I could walk fairly comfortably, Joch only had about a hand's width of space on either side. His sleeves brushed the sides of the wall as we walked. I was glad enclosed spaces didn't bother me.

It wasn't long before Joch stopped again and looked over his shoulder at me, his eyes glittering in the dark. "This is a good place to stop for a moment," he said in a low voice.

"Where are we now?"

He hesitated, then lifted a hand to tap lightly on the wall. "See for yourself," he said.

There was a slit in the wall. I could tell from the tiny beam of light flickering through. I pushed up on my toes to try to see through, but it was just a hair too tall for me to get a good look. "It's too high."

He chuckled. "I suppose you wouldn't be able to see much anyway. It's angled down so you can't see it from the other side. This one is more so you can hear what's going on in the room outside."

My eyes widened. "Where are we?"

"Just outside the throne room."

I became intently aware of my heart beating loudly in my chest. "Outside?"

I could feel rather than see him nod. "Near the main entrance, where guests would gather before entering." He looked through the slit. "I don't see or hear anyone now, but it's usually quite busy—and noisy. A good place to pick up gossip."

"Is there anything to see inside the room itself?"

"You could say that."

We turned a corner and I couldn't help but gasp. The passage was lit up with moonlight streaming in from large rectangular windows. "How?" I wondered aloud, walking up to the first one. "How could we not notice something like this?"

He didn't say anything, but it didn't take

long for me to piece it together on my own. I ran through the layout of the room in my mind, quickly figuring out where we were, and what was on the wall separating us from the room.

"The mirrors."

He gave me a wry grin. "The mirrors," he confirmed.

"We use some of these mirrors ourselves," I confessed, thinking of the mirrors in the dining hall, the ones Aiden and I used to see the court while we ate behind the divider. "But I had no idea these were here."

"The lighting has to be just right for them to work—another reason we can't use lanterns in here. But they're scattered all over the palace."

"Show me."

He lead me on a tour through the bowels of the palace until my eyes ached and I began to stumble. He saw and suggested we call it a night.

"That might be for the best," I admitted. The last thing I needed was to trip and fall, making noise and drawing attention. "Do we have to leave through the portrait as well?"

"There are two other exits I know of, but the portrait is closest to your quarters."

There was some comfort in that, and I made a mental note to have him show me the other exits. "Then let's go."

We parted ways outside the Hall of Portraits, and though Aiden probably would have preferred me to have Joch escorted back, it was late and I was tired, and I doubted Joch wanted anything more than his own bed at the moment.

After that, we met the next two nights to map out the rest of the passages. They spread through an impressive area of the palace, each new corridor making my stomach clench. And it seemed nearly all the mirrors in the palace were two-way.

"I'm never going to look at a mirror the same way again," I muttered, wiping away the cold sweat from the back of my neck.

Joch gave me a sympathetic look but didn't say anything.

Once I was more familiar with the layout

and less likely to trip over anything or make noise, we began meeting during the day. First, very early in the morning, then later and later, then whenever I could spare, with or without Joch.

The people in the palace had a lot to say when the royal siblings weren't in earshot.

Serving girls who thought Evie was either an inspiration or an embarrassment. Courtiers who thought the prince was a lovesick fool, too young or inexperienced, or too distracted to rule.

Chefs who were frustrated with lack of organization when there was too much food or not enough because the prince didn't care enough to properly manage the kitchens.

Physicians who were more curious about than afraid of the poison that still plagued my parents.

Suddenly I had a dozen more people to be worried about. I had a lot to tell Aiden.

Chapter Sixteen

$\mathcal{E}$vie had been making herself scarce ever since I returned with Joch, but our paths finally crossed after about a week. Normally Joch was glued to my side, but we had a rare morning apart as I commanded him to catch up on his sleep while I caught up with the noble ladies I'd been neglecting. I'd insisted Evie accompany me, a decision for which I was very grateful. Sometime the noble ladies had riveting discussions, but they didn't seem interested in discussing anything of significance today. As much I enjoyed simply chatting with the ladies, my mind was a bit too distracted to care about Lady Mariana's mother's sudden interesting in cooking with the servants or Lady Pippa's new horse. Apparently Aiden had taken my suggestion to heart and made an effort to introduce Evie to more of the court, so she was familiar with the ladies and could easily help entertain them.

"I'm completely exhausted now," she confessed afterward once we were alone in my rooms.

"You did beautifully," I assured her. "There will be fewer questions once the novelty has worn off."

"Only to start back up again once Aiden and I are officially engaged."

My ears perked up and I turned back to her, dropping the papers I'd been looking at on my desk. "Officially engaged?" I repeated.

She ducked her head. "He asked at the Masquerade last year, and I told him no. There'd been too many secrets between us and we needed to build the trust back up again, so I told him to ask again in a year."

"It hasn't been a year yet."

"No, but it seems we didn't need as much time as we thought. I think he's going to ask me again soon."

"Oh?"

"For as long as he kept his real identity from me, he's terrible at keeping anything from me now. Which is a good thing, I think," she hurried to say. "But it also means I can tell when he's planning something."

"Is he planning something?"

"His overprotectiveness is at an all-time height, which I understand, but he also keeps cutting himself off mid-sentence. Like he's planning something and hasn't included me in it, but has forgotten that I don't already know."

"Like he's planning for the future but doesn't want to assume you'll be a part of it?"

She nodded. "But honestly I don't think either of us could see a future without the other now. Delaying the engagement is simply delaying the inevitable. And I think he's starting to see that too."

"I think he saw that a long time ago."

She opened her mouth to say something to

that, but we were interrupted by a knock at my door, one I recognized as the guards' code for my brother.

"Speaking of my brother," I muttered. I wanted more time with Evie, but apparently more time with my future sister was too much to ask when it was time she could be spending with him instead.

The door opened, revealing not only Aiden but Joch as well. Neither looked happy about it, and I shuddered to think about what Aiden could have said to him without me there to soften the blow.

"Evie?" Aiden held out an arm for her, which she readily accepted with a warm smile.

"Hello to you too, brother, dear," I teased.

He blinked and looked at me, as if he'd already forgotten I was here and this was, in fact, my room. "Sorry, Bianca. My mind is in a million different places today."

"I'm sure it is," I said as I exchanged a knowing glance with Evie. I ushered them both out the door. "And I'm sure not one of them is with your little sister. Now go."

I watched them leave as Joch took Evie's

place in one of the plush chairs. "We're going to have to keep an eye on them tonight," I announced.

"Oh? And why's that?"

I simply said, "Aiden's too distracted to keep his eyes on anything but her."

"I don't blame your brother for being so wary of me, you know," Joch said as we resumed our posts in the dark passageway. I'd noticed he was much more likely to talk to me in the dark, and I felt a sort of sweet thrill at his progress. It was rare for him to start the conversation.

"There's a difference between being wary and being outright hostile," I pointed out.

"I deserve hostility."

I exhaled loudly. "Look, I understand that—"

"No, you don't," he interrupted, his voice as sharp as the look he gave me. "You don't understand me. You barely know me. You have this impossibly optimistic outlook on life, and it's clouding your vision. I've killed people. Innocent people. And I don't regret it. That's not something you can just ignore."

"I'm not trying to ignore it; I'm trying to help you move past it!" I exclaimed. "Something horrible happened, I know that much. I don't need to know more than that. But I also know that you can't keep —"

He interrupted me again, impatient and insistent. "I killed Evie's father to get his masks, so I could get close to your brother and kill him. I was told he was the reason Ta—" He stumbled over the name and took a breath before continuing. "The reason Tatiana was gone. But I was lied to. Tatiana left on her own, and I was used as nothing more than a means to an end. And now she's dead and I have nothing." He exhaled. "There, now you know."

"You don't have nothing," I insisted. "You have a chance to start over. But you can't start your future if you keep living in the past. I understand that you've been through something horrible and you need time to heal, but healing is an active process. Nothing is going to change if you don't fight for it."

He scoffed at me but didn't say anything.

"I'm not saying pretend like it didn't happen, but can't you fight for the life you would have had if things had been different? Don't you want that?"

"There's no point in wanting what I can't have."

"It's better than not wanting anything at all." I pursed my lips in annoyance. "Humor me. From today forward, I want you to act like you're already the person you want to be."

He was silent for a long moment, and I couldn't tell if he was considering my proposal or simply trying to find a polite way to tell me I was being naive and ridiculous.

When he spoke, his voice was soft. "I don't know who I want to be."

"That's all right," I said quickly, excited he was giving this a chance. "I can help you figure it out. Think about who you admire and why you admire them. Think about who you hate and why you hate them. Choose the good and reject the bad."

He leaned back against the wall, looked to the ceiling, and chuckled. "You make it sound so simple, like picking the best berries out of a batch and throwing away the rotten ones."

"Well, the concept is the same."

He turned to look at me. "Is that how you see everything? Pick out the good and reject the bad?"

I was about to deny it but hesitated. "I wouldn't say I reject the bad, exactly, but I do pick out the good, I suppose. I just believe there's good everywhere if you look hard enough."

His look turned skeptical.

"Sometimes I have to look very hard," I conceded. "And sometimes bad is bad with no reason I can see. But I can always find a way to work something good out of it."

When he didn't reply, I bumped his shoulder with mine. "I have excellent eyesight. Don't worry. I'll help you find what you're looking for."

He turned away to look through the peep-hole again, but I saw his smile.

It flickered and disappeared quickly, though, as he said, "We've got company."

"Is it Aiden?"

He gave me a surprised look. "How did you know?"

I grinned. "I had a suspicion he would come here tonight."

We were outside the Hall of Portraits again, and I just knew Aiden would bring Evie here tonight. They had several haunts in the palace where they spent their time, like the gardens or in Evie's workspace by the Masking Rooms, but this room had a certain air of significance to it with all the kings and queens of the past staring down at you. This was a room where decisions were made.

A quarter hour later, the young couple was finally officially engaged.

Chapter Seventeen

reparations for the happy couple's engagement ball began right away. Normally my mother would oversee much of the planning, but she and the king were still weak. At Aiden's insistence, they'd left the palace for a country estate where they could recover in peace.

That meant the work fell to Aiden and Evie. Aiden was already extremely busy with running the country and Evie was immediately overwhelmed with all that had to be done, so really, the work fell to me.

Luckily, I was not afraid of work and I loved big celebrations.

Everything else fell to the background as I planned for the occasion. I spent most of my time in my rooms, writing letters and lists and seating charts. I left all efforts to discovering our poisoner to Joch.

But that didn't mean we still didn't spend time together, and that led to some awkward moments with Evie, as she was almost always with me to help with the planning.

The first time they were in a room together, neither said a word to the other. Evie looked at him once and then ignored him for the rest of the afternoon while Hachi growled softly the entire time Joch was in the room. Joch left as soon as he was done with the task I'd assigned him.

I asked her if she wanted me to make sure he wasn't in the room when she was, but she told me not to worry about it. "You trust him not to hurt me—or you. I just need to get used to him being near and to who he is now. If what you've told me is true, I'd probably want to put the past behind me as much as he does."

Aiden was so lucky to have her.

The second time, she still didn't speak to Joch but did at least look at him. She watched him carefully, almost curiously. And he was as docile as I'd ever seen him.

The afternoons began to blur together, and though they never spoke and the atmosphere were always tense and they still kept their distance from one another, they seemed to grow used to each other.

Soon, everything was coming together. Musicians, dancers, singers—we would have the best in the country and as many from abroad as could make the sudden trip. The only thing I required of Aiden was the final approval of the menu. He enjoyed food, and I wanted this meal to be special.

We sat in my suite looking over the final menu, with Evie at my desk writing out invitations. "So, what do you think?" I asked him.

He nodded thoughtfully. "You have a good memory for all my favorites."

I smiled. "It's not hard when you'll eat just about anything."

"Ah, but there's a difference between eating

and enjoying. And what you've got planned looks truly enjoyable."

I laughed, and Evie smiled at us before returning to frown at her penmanship and shaking out her hand. We'd spent many hours practicing, and she quickly learned to hate the tradition that the bride handwrite each invitation.

"Evie likes everything as well?" Aiden asked, looking to her.

"Evie doesn't know what half the things are but is willing to trust her fiancé's judgment," she said, not looking up, her concentration completely on her calligraphy. He watched her with such affection it made my heart hurt at the sweetness.

I cleared my throat.

Aiden looked back at me, sheepish. "Sorry. It's still sinking in."

I just shook my head fondly. "So everything has your approval, then?"

He hesitated. "I do have one minor change. For the seafood dish, instead of the flounder, I want pufferfish. From Nishima."

"Pufferfish," I repeated, confused. "The

'extremely poisonous if not prepared correctly'
pufferfish. That pufferfish?"

"Yes.

I sighed. "Aiden, please. You don't think
you are tempting fate by serving pufferfish?"

"We need to show the court we are not
afraid."

"Fearless or reckless?"

"It is a calculated risk." He met my eyes and
did not look away.

Pufferfish went on the menu.

Somehow, everything managed to fall into
place and the night of the ball arrived. We
would begin with an elaborate seven-course
meal, then dance until morning. We wore
our finest whites, but only a half mask for the
occasion, since we would be eating with the
court tonight instead of behind our screen.

It still took hours for Carmine and Rufina
to dress me and do my hair. Under the strict
supervision of trusted guards, a pair of maids
I'd known for years were entrusted with Evie's
care, and I was excited to see her. For all her

artistry, she normally dressed quite simply. I don't think she wanted to draw attention to herself.

When I saw her, I knew that she would have all the attention tonight. She looked lovely, with white pearls in her dark curls and a full gown of green and gold and more pearls sewn into the bodice and at the wrists of her sleeves. She wouldn't wear whites until she was married, but the pearls were a nice touch.

Aiden looked just as dashing in his royal robes and I was sure I heard a maid sigh as he walked by.

And to my surprise, Joch was dressed as richly as a noble. I'd ordered clothes for him, but somehow never really pictured them on him.

He looked handsome.

Very handsome.

"Evening, princess," he greeted with a short bow. I nodded, my throat suddenly dry. "Shall we?" he asked, holding out his arm.

I cleared my throat. "Thank you."

And thus we began the processional to the banquet hall.

Aiden was of course seated at the head table with me on his right and Evie to his left. Joch would have been able to sit with us as a guest of honor, but Aiden wasn't willing to grant him that courtesy title, so instead he stood slightly behind me and to my right. He would taste my food, then wait patiently for the next course. Normally, he would test the food in the kitchen right before it was delivered, but Aiden wanted to make a statement tonight. If Joch was still hungry after the meal, he could sit at one of the lower tables and eat there. Since we were served first and the room was quite packed, he would have plenty of time to eat if he wanted.

I knew he wouldn't and I planned to have food sent to his room later.

"Thank you for coming here tonight," Aiden said, addressing the room once everyone was settled. "The king and queen would also thank you, but they are still away, tending to their health. We thank those of you who have asked after them. They are recovering well and we hope to see them in Venesia again soon. Luckily, my beloved sister, the princess Bianca, is able to honor us with her presence on this special night. It is my pleasure to officially introduce you to someone else very dear to me, someone a few of you may have already met." He looked fondly at Evie, reaching a hand down to her. She took it and rose with a grace that made me proud. I knew how nervous she was of looking like a clumsy fool. "My intended. We are officially engaged to be married, and thus she has been given the title of princess until we are wed. So I present to you, Princess Evelina."

The court applauded, though with the masks I could not tell how many were genuinely pleased with the engagement. I was sure my brother left a few broken hearts behind him.

"Now, let's celebrate!"

Dozens of servants carrying silver platters entered the room. They looked to our table for the signal to begin serving. The prince must be served first, and any other member of the royal family, before anyone else could eat. Our servants made quick work of placing in front of us small silver bowls of delicious smelling cream soup topped with chives.

Aiden dipped his spoon in and seemingly ate without any thought. "Delicious," he said, then motioned to Joch. "Now your turn."

"Shall I fetch my own spoon or will the princess's suffice?" Joch asked dryly.

Everyone was waiting for me to eat, and my stomach was growing impatient with the warm, creamy smell so near. "Use mine. It will take too long for a servant to fetch another."

"If your brother has no objections."

"Just eat the soup," Aiden said, his mouth tight.

"You're enjoying this, aren't you?" I muttered to Joch under my breath.

He offered me a wry smile as he spooned a small portion of the soup into his mouth.

Then he started to choke and my heart stopped.

Chapter Eighteen

*A*t first, I thought he might have just playing a terrible joke, to tease Aiden, but then I remembered that Joch didn't really play, and there was real fear in his eyes.

"Aiden!" I cried for help as I grabbed Joch's arm and tried to steady him as he pawed at his own throat. He'd already stopped coughing and was barely producing any sound at all, just a frantic gasping as he struggled to suck in air.

Aiden took one look and sprang into

action. He reached for a vial he'd hidden in his robes and pulled the cork out with his teeth while grabbing Joch's face with his free hand. Joch instinctively jerked back, but Aiden held firm and managed to pour the honey-brown liquid into Joch's mouth. Aiden clamped his hand over Joch's mouth and waited for Joch to swallow.

"It'll burn, but it'll keep you alive," Aiden said.

I felt helpless. I felt like even my heart was holding its breath, like no part of me could breathe until he did.

"Please," I whispered. Joch's eyes shot to mine, wide and more panicked than I'd ever seen them. I couldn't look away, not even to see if Aiden thought the antidote was working the way it should. Looking away would feel like abandoning him.

Waiting for him to breath again, the room shrank to only us. I forgot about the crowds of nobles watching our every move. I didn't hear every spoon drop as they began to panic. In that moment, I didn't care about anyone but him.

And I started to realize just how much I cared.

Before I could comprehend what that meant, he blinked and inhaled sweet air that could finally reach his lungs. He started blinking rapidly, his eyes wet as he sucked in more air and his body began to relax.

I finally exhaled.

"Act as if nothing has happened," Aiden murmured to us, and I turned my head sharply to argue. He'd sat back down as we waited for the antidote to take hold, his back straight. His expression was determined and proud, but I didn't miss how tightly he held Evie's hand in his lap—behind the table and away from the eyes of the court. He gave it one more squeeze before releasing it and standing.

"Bring the entire kitchen staff in here at once," he commanded. "Anyone who does not come will be Marked and exiled immediately."

The room broke into excited whispers, but silenced after a moment as Aiden stared the nobles down.

I watched nervously as Joch's breathing returned to normal and the color returned to his face. He watched the soup still in front of him, as if it would spring to life and attack him again.

The kitchen staff began filing in with various reactions as guards ushered them forward to stand in the center of the room where the entertainers performed only moments before. The servers all looked terrified, most of them young, all of them knowing their livelihoods were at stake. The chefs and cooks looked distracted, many of them throwing nervous glances back the way the came, probably worried about the food that was supposed to be in the process of being prepared and served. The head chef looked angry.

"Would one of you," Aiden began, his voice cold as iron, "care to explain how the princess was nearly poisoned just now?"

They gasped as one. Even the head chef's anger flickered into confusion. He didn't do it. I didn't know whether to be relieved at his innocence or worried that we were still in the dark.

The staff members looked to one another, but no one spoke up.

"Well?" he prompted.

"Spoon," Joch rasped, and every head turned to him.

"What?" I placed a steadying hand on his arm.

He nodded toward the spoon, which had fallen to the table next to the bowl of soup. I reached for it, confused, and turned it over in my hands. The inside had turned black.

I reached for Aiden's spoon to see if his would do the same when dipped in the soup.

It remained silver. I tested Evie's as well, but it remained an unchanged, gleaming silver.

"The poison was on the spoon," I said, bewildered. That was how I could be so specifically targeted. The places were set before anyone arrived, and in the flurry of activity, it would be easy for someone to switch my spoon out for a poisoned one.

"Who was in charge of setting the princess's place?" Aiden asked the wide-eyed crowd of servants. No one was surprised when no one stepped forward to answer. Aiden directed his gaze at the kitchen mistress, the one in charge of all the servers.

"My prince, I truly do not know," she simpered. "There was so much to do and so many people coming in and out in preparation—anyone could have done it."

He gave her a long, hard look.

"In your opinion, then, is the rest of the meal safe to eat? Assume your life depends on it."

"Y-yes, my prince," she stuttered.

Aiden looked at the head chef.

"Yes, my prince," he replied as well, looking somewhat less angry and more shamed.

"You swear on your life that the remaining courses will be safe to eat?"

"Yes, my prince. I will taste every dish myself, and bring out new, cleaned silverware for the entire court."

"Then we shall continue our celebration," Aiden said with an air of dark humor, daring anyone to challenge him. "Though I find myself in need of a new poison tester. Just to be safe."

At least he wasn't forcing Joch to do it. That meant we could likely leave soon.

"I will do it, my prince." Lady Mariana's mother's voice carried throughout the chamber as she rose to her feet. The Lady Isabella was a tall and dark beauty like her daughter, and equally as vain and eager for power. That she would volunteer meant they must see how gaining Aiden's favor would benefit them.

This was good, Aiden needed this. When he looked to me for my opinion, I nodded.

"Very well. Thank you for your willing sacrifice," he said with a slight bow of his head. She curtseyed as deep as the table allowed with dignity.

The guards filed the massive number of staff back to the kitchen and conversation slowly returned to the chamber, slow and hesitant at first, then quickly snowballing to the level it was before the whole affair happened. Aiden motioned for musicians to resume their entertainment, and if it weren't for Joch nervously rubbing his throat, I wouldn't have guessed anything was amiss.

"How long do we have to stay?" I asked Aiden softly.

"Through the meal," he replied, his chin still held high. I made a sound of protest and he softened ever so softly. "You don't have to eat anything," he conceded gently. "But we need to put on a strong front. Show them we aren't afraid." He paused, then said, "Even if we are."

I felt guilty for wanting to leave. Of course he had to stay, and of course he wanted to leave just as much as I did. But he was determined to do whatever he felt needed to be done, which was in this case, despite everything, eat and dance and celebrate his new engagement.

The night dragged on. As happy as I was for Aiden, I was too worried about Joch. Lady Isabella was true to her word and tasted my food, but Joch insisted on tasting it as well. I barely managed ten bites for the rest of the evening.

Finally, it was time to move to the ballroom for dancing, and I could slip away. I would need to make a few appearances so I couldn't go too far, but at least people would stop staring at my every move. My brother and Evie lead the way, and I followed close behind as protocol demanded. Joch wasn't ranked high enough to accompany me, but I couldn't find it in me to care at the moment. I hooked my arm into his and gave him a quick nod, motioning for him to come with me.

The court whispered, but they would be whispering about many things tonight; one more couldn't hurt. Once the ballroom was full, the royal couple started the first dance, and all eyes were on them.

"Come with me," I whispered to Joch and pulled him away from the crowd and out onto a balcony. The summer night was cool, a welcome reprieve from the already warm ballroom. I could finally ask him, "Are you okay?"

He chuckled, then winced. "Throat hurts," he rasped.

I clicked my tongue in sympathy. "I'm sure it does. You'll need to rest it for a few days, I'm sure. No talking whenever possible. Think you'll be able to handle that?"

"I'll manage." He seemed distant, but I suppose almost dying would do that.

We stood there in silence, leaning against the cold marble and looking out at the gardens.

I was in no hurry to return to the ball and I wouldn't be missed for a while yet.

Or so I thought, until Aiden approached us as soon as the first set ended, his attention solely on Joch.

"I need to speak to you."

Chapter Nineteen

Those words combined with that determined expression rarely preceded a
pleasant conversation.

"Aiden," I warned him.

He shook his head. "No, I need to say this."
He took a deep breath and faced Joch directly.
Joch looked back with a cautious eye. "Thank
you."

Whatever Joch had been expecting, apparently it wasn't that. "What?" he asked in his
new raspy voice.

"Don't speak. You need to rest your throat," Aiden said automatically and then hesitated again. "Thank you for being willing to risk your life for my sister. Maybe you're not going to kill her after all."

"Aiden," I chided, but he shook his head again.

"That's as much as I'm willing to concede. I still don't like him and I still don't trust him. But he did well tonight and he deserves my thanks for it."

He excused himself and returned to the ball, leaving Joch and I slightly dumbfounded.

"I haven't thanked you yet either," I finally said, tracing a vein in the short marble balcony wall. How does one thank someone for taking poison for them?

He tried to scoff, but it turned into an awful coughing noise, and I looked at him in alarm. He waved my concern aside. "It's fine," he whispered.

"You should really stop talking."

He gave me a weak smile instead.

Compared to dinner, the rest of the night was extremely uneventful. Thanks to our careful planning, everything worked out as it should and there wasn't much left for me to do but watch it happen. I made the occasional appearance and danced when asked (which was only twice—I think Aiden had something to do with that) and left as early as I could manage.

The days following a ball like that were almost always spent in recovery. Court was supposed to be quiet, catching up on sleep, and maybe spreading a few new pieces of gossip, depending on how scandalous it was.

Not this time.

This time, it seemed as if the frenzied energy of that night would never go away. I dined with the court the following evening at Aiden's request and then took the rest of my meals in my rooms. When I ate with them, the entire hall seemed to hold their breath with every bite, and I couldn't bear it.

Instead, I took advantage of my time to refocus my efforts on finding whoever was so determined to poison me. I knew now we could cross the head chef off the list of suspects, and none of the servants seemed to have motive to be so dedicated.

Joch and I resumed patrolling the passages together, though we didn't speak much while his throat continued to heal. We tried writing messages on paper, but it was so dim that reading them was too much work.

It wasn't long before I was feeling too cooped up to spend any time crouched in the dark passages. Two weeks after the ball, the hot summer sun blazed overhead and I wanted to go outside.

The gardens were lush and green this time of year, and we weren't the only ones to take advantage of the nice weather. Nobles were scattered throughout the winding gardens, admiring the marble statues and catching up on the latest gossip. Ladies hid under pale parasols as they wandered to and fro, and I envied their lazy afternoon strolls. I had a different goal in mind when we set out to the extensive gardens. Joch and I wanted to visit the herbal gardens.

They were further from the palace, past the pleasure gardens where the nobles congregated, and the long walk gave me time to gather my thoughts.

"Did you find out what kind of poison was used on my spoon?" I asked Joch once we were out of earshot of the other.

"I have a few suspicions," he answered. His voice was almost back to normal, but it wore out quickly and still had a slight rasp to it. His already succinct answers were cut even shorter. "I'll be looking for mushrooms."

We grew dozens of varieties. "Any in particular?"

"Poison ones."

I stumbled, missing a step. Was that a joke? He pulled ahead of me so I couldn't see his face, and when I caught up again, it was perfectly blank. I stared at him until he looked back at me and flashed the smallest grin.

It was a joke.

A smile stretched across my face and I decided to take his positive attitude as a sign that we'd find something good on our outing.

I led him to the long greenhouse, where enough mushrooms were grown to supply the palace, and a gardener met us at the entrance.

"Can I help you with anything, princess?" She was a stout, middle-aged woman with a vibrant green mask dotted with silver. I was not very familiar with the servants who worked outdoors, but she seemed comfortable with her surroundings, if a bit nervous at my visit.

"We'd like to inspect the mushrooms, please."

"Of course. Is . . . is something wrong to give you reason for an inspection?"

"Call it a whim," I said, following her inside. It was dark and humid and warm, the perfect condition for the flourishing mushrooms. They were grown in wooden crates filled with dirt, stacked on top of one another, and there must have been hundreds of them in neat rows, with the mushroom heads poking out.

I recognized portobellos, blue oysters, and wine caps, but there were a handful of varieties I didn't know by sight. The gardener patiently described each species, but I remember very little of what she said, too impatient to move on to the next one as soon as I recognized a name from a dish.

"And these over here?" I gestured to a short stack of much smaller crates practically hidden in a corner but surprisingly clean.

"We're experimenting with new growing methods and varieties, and those are our testers. We keep them further away so they don't accidentally breed with the established mushrooms."

I shared a quick glance with Joch and then asked, "May I?"

"Of course, princess."

I held my breath as Joch carefully inspected them, looking for his poisonous friends, but it didn't take long for him to shake his head at me. "They're perfectly innocent."

I released my breath, annoyed at my disappointment. I shouldn't want to find poisonous mushrooms in our gardens, but it would have been such a big step in the right direction.

"Thank you for showing us around," I told the gardener, who seemed all too relieved to say farewell.

"The grounds are huge," I pointed out as we walked through more of the garden, just to look around. "You could grow mushrooms anywhere."

"I suppose."

"But?"

"But that would have been the most reliable place to grow them, and the easiest to hide."

"Maybe whoever used them doesn't really know how to grow them. Maybe they bought them."

"That would look awfully suspicious, buying poisonous mushrooms," he said.

"Money can buy silence as easily as mush-rooms. You just need the right amount."

He didn't have a reply for that.

Chapter Twenty

Everything seemed to be leading to dead ends and I was growing tired of it. I was going through letters from friends abroad when I remembered the mysterious fire that burned down the barn in Nishima. It seemed odd that I hadn't received any update on it and I asked my guards. "Have you heard anything from Felix about what caused that fire?"

Rufina and Carmine exchanged looks. They knew something. "What?" I demanded.

"I thought he would have told her by now," Carmine said to Rufina, biting her lip.

"Clearly not, so you should tell me now." My voice was flat and extremely unamused. They knew how upset I became when they kept information from me. I felt betrayed.

The pair seemed to be silently arguing over who would break the news to me. Carmine lost.

"We had instructions when we left Venesia," she began carefully.

"Instructions from who?"

She paused again before answered, and I knew before she spoke the words.

"The prince."

"What did he say?" I asked with clenched teeth.

"He didn't want you to be away for very long," Rufina finally spoke up. "And he said that if the Chameleon was taking too long, or seemed resistant, then to . . . well . . ."

I was stunned. "You started the fire?"

They both nodded glumly. "We made sure everyone else was away, including the animals. We never expected you to go in after him."

"You started the fire." The words kept echoing in my head.

"To protect you."

"Ha!"

Carmine stepped forward to try to comfort me but I recoiled. "To protect you the best way he knows how. He—"

I ignored her. How dare Aiden go behind my back like this. How dare he not tell me when it was my own life and my own choices on the line. "Where is he now?"

"I-I'm not sure," Carmine said, looking nervously to Rufina. "Perhaps in his office? Or in the Masking Rooms with Evie?"

I marched down to his office, hoping to find him before my anger faded. He deserved the full brunt of it. His guards were outside the door, and they were quick to open the doors for me.

Aiden was at his desk with papers spread out before him. He looked puzzled as I stomped in. "Bianca?"

"Is it true, what my guards just told me?" I demanded.

"What?" He looked behind me for the guards in question, but I didn't know or want to wait for them to answer if they were there.

"Did you instruct them to kill Joch if it took too long to convince him or if he was unwilling to help?"

Aiden's face hardened. "Yes."

"How could you?! I thought you trusted me! I thought—"

"You are a child!" Aiden shouted back, coming around the desk to tower over me.

"You were always the childish one!" I retorted. "You're the one who ran away from his problems and left me to be the responsible one. You're the one—"

"I'm the one who's been told as long as I can remember that one day the entire country will rely on me. That if people die because of lack of food or because of war, it will be my fault. I'm the one with—"

"And I don't have responsibility? I'm the face of our family and country when I go abroad."

"You may be the pretty face, but I'm supposed to be the heart and brain. Once I'm in power, if I fail in any way, our country fails."

"And yet you still ran away?"

"I needed time away from the crushing weight of it all!"

We glared at each other. My head pounded as the depth of his betrayal sunk in.

"I never knew you were so selfish. I'm ashamed to call you my brother."

I couldn't look at him anymore. I needed to get out, to get some air. A summer storm was rolling in and the thick air crackling with the promise of thunder and lightning did nothing to ease my temper. I wanted to be alone, but there was nowhere in the palace I could go without been watched or interrupted, especially with my white mask on. And my room held too many memories of time spent with him. Memories now tainted with the uncertainty of if he'd ever meant it when he said he trusted me.

Frustrated, I decided memories were better than curious and gossipy servants, and retreated.

Joch was waiting for me there. "Do you still want to—wait, Princess, are you all right?"

"No," I said abruptly and went inside, wiping my face clean of any tears that may have escaped and suddenly glad for my mask. He cautiously followed me, and I didn't know if I wanted to send him away or not. Perhaps his company was what I needed right now.

I told him what Aiden had done, that he was responsible for the fire at the stables.

To my surprise, he seemed unfazed. "I thought it might have been."

"You did?"

He shrugged and sat at my desk, watching me. Meanwhile, my fury with Aiden was still burning, building higher the more I thought about what he'd done and what he'd said to me. I paced my room, unable to sit still, while Joch watched from my desk, picking through the bowl of apples that had been brought up earlier.

"Why aren't you as angry as I am about this?"

"I expected it. I'm well aware how much he hates me, and I've learned how much he loves you. He'd hate to hear this, but we're not that different when it comes to the lengths we'll go to protect someone."

I paused for just a moment, then resumed my pacing. "It's no excuse. He's been treating me like a child ever since he's become regent, as if he wasn't the one always running off and shirking his duties. He doesn't trust my judgment and he doesn't trust me. I'm tired of the way he's trying to control every aspect of my life!"

Joch let me rant without comment. Then he said with that hint of dry humor I'd grown familiar with, "If you want to rebel, I know a way to start small."

He handed me an apple.

Chapter Twenty-one

I never thought biting into an apple would feel daring, but I could not deny the thrill as I grinned at Joch and took a large bite.

It tasted like autumn, fresh and crisp and everything an apple should be.

But then it had a bitter, metallic aftertaste.

Something was wrong. My tongue felt heavy.

Joch sensed it immediately, straightening and looking at me with alarm in his eyes. "Princess?"

I couldn't speak, my lips and throat felt numb, and the adrenaline morphed into something foreign as the numbness began to spread. My knees buckled as the emptiness reached my legs, and Joch scrambled to catch me as I fell.

"Bianca!"

I felt like I was slipping into a dream and my eyes fell shut. He'd used my name, a distant part of my mind registered. He'd never done that before.

"Send for her brother! Now!" Joch shouted at the guards outside my door.

I couldn't see him, but I could feel him. He placed one hand at my throat, feeling my slowing pulse, the other hand cradling my head against his chest.

"Please," he whispered, "don't you leave me too."

Too?

I kept waiting to lose consciousness, but such relief never came. This was some kind of waking slumber poison. I couldn't move, but I could hear, smell, and feel everything going on around me.

I heard Aiden come in, shouting at Joch.

Don't shout at him, I wanted to say. *He couldn't have known.*

Instead, mute, I was yanked out of Joch's arms.

Chapter Twenty-two

I drifted in and out of awareness. I didn't hurt, but I felt exhausted, no matter how much I slept. I felt like I was slowly fading into nothing, like I was just existing in a shell of a body until the tethers that held me eroded away to nothing.

I don't know how much time passed, but Aiden was by my side almost constantly. He didn't speak much, but I could feel his presence.

Joch tried to come, but he had to time his visits to when Aiden wasn't there. The first time he and Aiden were in the same room, Aiden tried to kill him.

"This is your fault," he growled and lunged at him. I heard the metallic ring of his dagger unsheathing and the thud of bodies hitting the wall, and for a terrible moment, I thought Aiden succeeded.

But miraculously, Joch spoke. "It is my fault," he said in a soft, defeated voice. "I'm the reason she ate the apple." He paused. "But you're the reason she even considered it."

There was a long pause. The longer it dragged on, the more helpless and frustrated I felt. My choices were my own. I didn't want them killing each other over them.

"Did you poison the apples?" Aiden finally asked.

"Look at me."

I knew the answer and it must have been written on Joch's face.

I think Aiden knew it too. He just didn't like it.

"Find out who did," he commanded. "I don't want to see you again until you do."

I heard Joch mutter something that

sounded like, "The feeling is mutual," and the soft click of the door opening and closing.

There were few visitors after that. Carmine and Rufina were often there, but as guards, not guests. Though I couldn't respond, Carmine would tell me the latest palace gossip, and Rufina would tell me stories. I drifted in and out of understanding but appreciated it nonetheless.

The most surprising guest was Lady Mariana and her mother. Their visit was strange from the start—they came without guards, and I didn't hear the door open. The latter wouldn't have been so strange if their entrance wasn't preceded by the sound of something heavy sliding across the floor. A sound frustratingly familiar but not one I could place immediately.

"I thought you said the poison would kill her," Mariana whispered. "She still looks quite alive."

In a sudden ringing of clarity, I remembered the sound. It was just like the one the painting of the palace gardens made at one of the exits to the secret passages. Then I remembered my mirror, and how it had been there as long as I could remember. Then I remembered the one-way glass.

They must have found more passages or another entrance to the ones that had been blocked. They'd been spying on me in my own rooms.

"Hush. It should have," Lady Isabella said. "And it when she doesn't wake up, it will. Do you see now what I have done for you?"

"It was foolish to come here simply to gloat."

"We're not here to gloat. We're here to see how much longer she has left."

I felt them come nearer and my stomach turned.

"Why? It looks like she won't last another day."

"I need to know when to strike at the prince's fiancée. He'll be too distracted by the princess's death to properly protect his intended."

"And then I will win him back." The sound of footsteps approached in the hall, and the two traitors retreated. "Quickly," Isabella said, and they disappeared behind the mirror.

I felt like I was dreaming. When Aiden came back, it was maddening not being able to tell him. For hours he sat by my side, reading books that had been brought to him about various poisons, but he tossed one after another aside, none of them apparently holding the answer that I did.

"Well?" he asked during Joch's next visit.

"The apple was infused with a higher concentration of the poison you give me each day."

A moment of silence paused before Aiden responded. "This is good news, isn't it? Why don't you look happy? Will the antidote work on her?"

"Probably," he said. "But she'll need all you have. There won't be any left for me."

I wanted to scream but still couldn't so much as blink.

"You're . . . volunteering? To give your portion up to her?"

"Yes."

"You'd do that? For her?"

"Of course."

Aiden sounded absolutely perplexed, and

Joch resigned but resolute. I desperately wished I could see their faces.

"One of your doctors is preparing it now. It should be ready soon."

Aiden didn't need to explain what would happen to Joch. They both knew perfectly well that without the antidote, the poison would kill Joch. It was not a quick-acting poison, but once it had been in his body for a day with nothing to counteract it, it would be too late stop it from taking over.

They waited in silence on either side of me. Aiden held my left hand with both of his as he hunched over the bed. Joch hesitated, then slipped my right hand into his, fingers intertwined. I couldn't even twitch my finger to give either of them some kind of reassurance.

The door creaked opened.

"My prince?" a guard asked for Aiden.

"Is the doctor here?"

The guard must have nodded, and I heard footsteps approach.

"My prince," the doctor said. "Since we don't know exactly how much poison she ingested, I don't know how much antidote she'll need. Too much won't hurt her, but too little could be as ineffective as nothing. I brought all we have."

I heard Joch take a deep breath.

Surely there's enough to save one dose for him, I wanted to plead. *Don't condemn him out of overprotection of me.*

"Joch," Aiden began, but didn't say anything more.

"Give it all to her."

"Are you sure?" Aiden's voice was grim.

"More sure of anything I've ever been before. She can't die. She just . . . can't." His voice broke on the last word. He cleared his throat. "Not if there's anything I can do. I swore I would keep her safe. I never go back on my word."

You fool. I wanted to cry, but I couldn't do that either.

"Very well. Will you prop her up?"

Joch complied, sitting beside me and wrapping an arm around me to lift my head and shoulders.

A cool glass cup was pressed to my lips, nudging my mouth open. Bitter, hot liquid poured down my throat, nearly choking me.

I coughed.

The heat raced throughout my body and I could feel the tethers snap back into place. I jerked back into consciousness, my eyes flying open.

The antidote was still on my lips. As soon as Joch came into focus beside me, I jerked him forward and pressed my lips to his.

I wasn't going to let him go so easily.

He froze at my touch but melted almost instantly, his lips returning my kiss.

I hadn't exactly imagined my first kiss to be a matter of life or death, but I was right in that it would be unforgettable.

"Bianca!"

I pulled back, remembering Aiden. I shot him a guilty, weak smile, before looking back to Joch.

"You're not going to die for me," I whispered, my throat dry and sore.

He blinked. "What?"

My eyes flickered to his lips as I cleared my throat. "I heard you. I heard everything while I was unconscious, but I heard you give up your antidote for mine. Your dose was so small you don't need much. It was the least I could do."

He still looked a little dumbstruck, like it hadn't really sunk in. I knew I couldn't have been that good a kisser.

Aiden cleared his throat and I guiltily turned to face him. I expected disapproval or anger on his face, but all I saw was relief. He opened his arms to me and I let go of Joch to lean into them.

"I'm sorry," I said, needing to start with an apology. Not for kissing Joch in front of him—though he probably didn't much appreciate that—but for the things I'd said. And for being reckless. And probably a few other things. "How mad are you right now?" I whispered.

He let out an exasperated laugh. "I'm just relieved to see you alive. I can't be mad about anything."

I pulled back to look him straight in the eye and then glanced at Joch, who looked a bit shocked.

"Truly?"

"Bianca," he started, then turned to address

Joch instead, his voice solemn. "Joch, I will never like you."

Joch opened his mouth to retort, but I silenced him with a look.

"But I would be a fool to deny that you want what's best for my sister. And if she can believe in you, and if Evie has forgiven you, I suppose I can try."

I beamed at him and hugged him again. He held me tight and continued to address Joch. "But don't think I won't still be watching your every move. Give me an excuse to hurt you and I will."

I groaned and gave him a gentle shove with my forehead. "Aiden."

"What kind of brother would I be if I didn't protect my little sister?" His tone was light, but his eyes were serious. I'd scared him.

"You're going to be as unbearably overprotective as ever now, aren't you?"

"You better believe it."

Chapter Twenty-three

You said you heard everything—what did you mean? Did you hear anything important?" Aiden spoke quickly, looking around as if he expected to fight again at any moment.

"Oh, yes." I shot a glance at the mirror, wondering if they were still watching me. I didn't want them knowing, but if they saw I was awake, we would need to act quickly. I doubted they would stay around much longer. "Remember the passages we found?" I directed my question to Joch while Aiden listened impatiently. "I found another one."

"While you were asleep?" Joch asked.

"There's one behind my mirror, and I'll bet that glass is no ordinary mirror."

Aiden looked horrified as Joch rose to inspect the mirror.

"How well do you know Lady Isabella and her daughter?" I asked Aiden. "Is there some history I don't know?"

"Did you know Mariana was the one Father picked for me to marry if I didn't find someone else at my masquerade?"

I gasped. "No! How come you never told me that?" It seemed a trivial thing to be upset over, given that he was happily engaged to Evie now, but I still felt a little insulted.

"Telling you would have made it more real. I didn't want to marry her. I didn't want to marry anyone, really, but knew I'd have to eventually. I just thought putting off telling you about it would mean I could put off marrying as well."

I groaned. "And when Isabella offered to be my replacement tester? You didn't think that was suspicious?"

"I thought she was trying to get back into the family's good graces. I knew they weren't pleased when I picked Evie. Why, what have they done?"

"'Weren't pleased' seems to be an understatement. They came through my mirror, and they were the ones that poisoned the apples, as well as everything else it seems."

Aiden leaned back, dumbfounded. "But that can't be true. You must have dreamed it."

"It was no dream," Joch spoke up from over by my mirror. "Look." He reached behind the golden frame with both hands, and after a faint click, shifted the entire mirror to reveal a dark opening. "There are latches hidden in the frame."

There was murder in Aiden's eyes, and for once, it wasn't directed at Joch. "They're both going to hang by morning."

"Wait." I placed a hand on his arm. "You need to publicly discredit them first or the court will rebel against you. They're a powerful family. You can't just execute them without proving what they've done."

"Is your word not enough?" he asked angrily.

I shook my head. "Not in this case. You need someone from outside the royal family."

He looked at Joch, but I was already shaking my head again. "And not him either. You barely believe him, and if word got out who he really was, you'd lose control of the court in no time."

"Then who?"

"Mariana and Isabella themselves. The court will believe no one else."

Aiden scowled. "That will take some planning. And time. If they've managed this much so far, they must be more dangerous and more clever than I thought."

"Please, plan away. And, yes, it will take time, but it will be better if you do this the right way than if you rush into sentencing them with nothing to back you up but the word of an ill sister. In the meantime, I would very much like a bath."

The pair of them seemed to suddenly remember that I'd been comatose and quickly excused themselves while Carmine and Rufina called for warm water and helped me bathe.

Once clean, I felt like a new person. I was still weak and annoyingly tired for someone who'd just spent days asleep, but I could feel my energy slowly returning.

"Joch is waiting for you in your sitting room," Carmine told me as she helped me into a simple pale blue dress. "Do you want me to tell him to give you more time to rest?"

I felt the ghost of his kiss at the sound of his name and blushed. "No, I want to see him."

She gave me a knowing look. "We'll give you some privacy then."

It seemed Joch had won my guards over as well as my brother.

I didn't expect to feel shy around him but at least the feeling appeared to be mutual. He pushed himself to his feet as I entered, but looked down after the briefest moment of eye contact.

"You're looking better already," he mumbled.

I smiled and lowered myself onto the settee next to him. "Thanks to you."

He smiled briefly but still seemed fascinated by the chair's arm.

"Why won't you look at me?"

He flinched, and reluctantly looked up. "I don't know. I don't know how to look at you after what happened in there." He didn't need to elaborate. I knew his tragic love history, and though I didn't know exactly his feelings for me or how deep they ran, I knew he must be confused. The last time he cared for someone, he'd been hurt badly. I think he knew me well enough to know that I wouldn't do that to him, at least not on purpose, but that didn't change the fact that anything between us would be complicated.

"I'm not mad about the kiss," I tried to reassure him. "Quite the opposite, actually. Even if it hadn't been a life or death situation."

He stared at me as the words sunk in.

"Really?" He allowed himself approximately two heartbeats of happiness before doubt and dismay clouded his face. "But you deserve someone better than me. Someone who isn't Marked."

I sighed. I hadn't worn a mask while I slept, but apparently he never got a good look at my face.

"You aren't the only one in this room who is Marked."

His eyes shot to mine, flooded with confusion as he quickly looked over my face, as if he could see through the white half-mask I wore now.

"People are Marked in order to keep track of them," I reminded him, "To punish them, yes, but also to make sure they cannot disappear behind a new mask." I took a deep breath, and without any further fanfare, removed my mask. "The royal family is also Marked. To ensure there are no imposters on the throne."

His eyes widened, taking in the small scar on my cheek in the shape of a crown. His hand moved to touch it, and I didn't shy away.

"Aiden has one too."

"I'd really rather not talk about your brother right now."

I laughed, pressing my hand to his, sandwiching it between my palm and my cheek. "Everyone is marked in their own way, Joch. Whether it's by official brands like ours, or by emotional pain or physical scars, no one can escape it. Is it so hard to think I would pick someone like you? Someone who has risked his life for me more than once? Someone who is loyal to a fault and brave and is trying to make the best of a terrible situation?"

He angled my face toward his and leaned closer.

"You make a better argument than I care to admit."

"Good."

Chapter Twenty-four

It didn't take long for Aiden to come up with a plan to catch Mariana and Isabella in their lies. He set his plans in motion by instructing the kitchens to start planning a celebratory dinner and issuing invitations to all the noble families in honor of my recovery.

"The palace is in a bit of a frenzy," Carmine informed me as she worked on my hair for the big dinner. "Especially so soon after the engagement dinner. Most people are happy to see you recover, but they're being worked very hard."

"We'll need to grant them some kind of holiday when this is all over," I mused, watching her work in the mirror. I sat at my vanity in my dressing room, far away from the full-length hidden door, which was now covered by a thin sheet. I didn't want to reveal I knew about the passage by destroying it, but I also couldn't stomach not knowing when someone was watching me. The sheet made it too difficult to see into the room.

"Knowing the culprit is caught will go a long way, as well. Everyone is on edge."

"Believe me, I know."

She offered me a sympathetic smile and gave my hair one last pat. "You're ready."

The walk to the banquet hall felt longer than usual, like I was walking to my own trial and not that of the noble ladies. Aiden was quiet, and Evie and Joch kept shooting nervous glances my way. I couldn't think of anything to say to reassure them, so I joined my brother's silence.

The banquet began much as the engagement ball had, with chatter and musicians as the guests filed in while Aiden and I watched, the main difference being that this time, we were the first to arrive so everyone could see me as soon as they entered the room.

Once Aiden was satisfied with attendance, he rose to speak.

"We want to thank you all for coming tonight. It is rare we have such happy events to celebrate so close to one another, but I think my sister's recovery warrants such a celebration."

Several nobles raised their glasses to me, and I smiled and nodded in their direction. My smile was tight and forced, but it was behind a full mask so no one would notice.

"Before we begin our feast tonight, we have someone else we wish to thank. Lady Isabella, please come before me."

There was a general murmur as she obeyed with a genteel smile on her lips.

"We wish to thank the Lady for her service in the absence of my sister's poison tester. As the court knows, it was truly a dangerous position." He gestured to a gloved servant, who came forward with a small box. Aiden took the box and then turned back to Isabella. "To repay you for what you have done."

If anyone else in the court noticed the hardness underlying his words, no one said anything.

Isabella graciously accepted the box and removed the lid. Inside were nestled two fine satin dancing slippers. They were a brilliant red, embroidered with white, and laced with string that my ribs recognized.

If she recognized it as well, she hid it. "Thank you, my prince."

"Put them on. Break them in tonight in honor of the princess," he insisted, looking to the servant again to assist her.

She hesitated and glanced at her daughter. Mariana seemed frozen to her seat.

Perhaps Isabella noticed the inside soles were coated in the same poison she'd put in the apples or that the heel was lined in the poison from my comb and likely to bite into her skin if the slightly-too-small new shoes wore through her stockings. The poisons had barely detectable scents, especially in the perfume-filled hall, but the fabric was slightly distorted from their application and she must have seen that something was unusual about them.

"Is there a problem?"

"O-of course not, my prince," she murmured, and allowed the servant to remove her own shoes and slip on the new ones.

She remained stone-faced and I almost thought Aiden's plan would fail—until she took a step. She winced and Mariana sprang from her seat, but dared not approach them with Aiden watching so closely.

"I will ask again," Aiden repeated; this time his voice was noticeably colder. "Is there a problem?"

She shook her head but continued to flinch with every step until she reached her seat, where Mariana watched her anxiously. Confused whispers sprang up around her as Aiden continued to stare her down.

Finally Mariana broke. "You've poisoned her!"

"Mariana, no!" Isabella rushed to silence her but it was too late.

"I've only returned to her what she has given to me."

It took a moment for his words to register among the court before they started to echo him, puzzling out the meaning.

"Funny that you immediately assume poison," he said, unmoving. "Could it be because you recognize the scent from when you poisoned a certain comb or a basket of apples? Or the laces from when you bribed a maid to try to suffocate the princess? Do you also fear your food will be tainted with the same poison you used on the king and queen?"

Nobles were standing now, protesting the accusations, but with every word, the two ladies' hard defense seemed to crumble. They knew that he knew. And they knew he would have no mercy.

They began to weep.

"I hereby sentence you both to hang for treason and attempted assassination of the king, queen, and princess."

Their heads both snapped up. "Both?" Isabella asked through her tears.

"I'm not foolish enough to let any of your kind of poison remain in my court after what your family has done."

Chapter Twenty-five

I didn't attend the execution, though the others did. Afterwards, Joch came to my rooms to tell me it was done.

"Thank you," I said in a soft voice. I wasn't exactly happy at the news—I could never be happy at the news of someone's death—but there was an undeniable sense of relief.

He hovered in the doorway.

"You can come in, you know."

He glanced over my shoulder to see the empty room behind me. "You're alone."

Doc was still stationed at my door, but he was the only one. Everyone else had wanted to be there for the execution, and it wasn't necessary for me to be so heavily guarded now. "For once," I said. "But the threat is gone now, so I expect the trend to continue."

He entered but didn't sit.

"I expect so."

I waited for him to continue, leafing through letters from curious and concerned friends abroad, but it seemed he was going to need some prodding. Even after all we'd been through, he was still rather quiet.

"Was there something you needed to talk to me about?"

"About the threat being gone . . . I suppose that means you don't need me anymore."

I set down the letters and gave him my full attention. "Just because that threat is gone doesn't mean I don't need you anymore. And, more important, it doesn't mean I don't want you anymore, either."

He looked so vulnerable that I rose and walked to him to take his hands in mine. He seemed to be debating something in his mind, so I gave him time to think over his words.

"So what does this mean for me? What am I supposed to do now?"

"Well," I began slowly. "What would you like to do?"

"I don't know my options. Have I earned my freedom?"

It stung a little that his first thought was to leave, that he felt caged here, but I kept my expression neutral, telling myself he was simply being practical. "I'm sure you have. I'll remind Aiden to make it official."

"But I could never go back to being myself. I never belonged here in the first place, and I'm tired of hiding behind masks."

"So you want to leave?"

"I don't want to stay in the palace. I don't know how you live with so many people watching you all the time."

"I'm used to it, I suppose. And it's not all the time. I do go out occasionally." He was making me nervous now. I didn't want him to leave, but I wasn't going to keep him here against his will. "So you want to leave the palace. Do you want to leave Venesia?"

"I don't know how I could stay. But . . ." He hesitated and I held my breath. "I don't want to leave you."

I exhaled and smiled, my heart pounding. "I don't want you to leave me either," I confessed. "But I want you to be happy. If I weren't part of the picture, what would you want to do? What would make you happy."

"It's hard to imagine."

I squeezed his hands. "I know. But try. You can go anywhere now. Where do you want to go?"

"I'd like to see my family again. Maybe return to glass working. I don't know that I want to keep being a guard, even if I'm good at it."

A reasonable desire, and not one I could deny him. "You can. There's nothing stopping you now."

"But I don't know if that would make me happy. Not if you weren't with me."

"Well." I leaned my head back as I stepped closer. "There's a simple enough solution for that, you know."

"What, bring you with me?" He laughed.

I didn't. Instead, I shrugged. "Why not? All you have to do is ask."

He stopped laughing. "I couldn't ask you to do that. You're a princess. You have duties here: you can't just run off."

"That is partly true. I do have duties and I am a princess. But many of those duties take me away from Venesia. And even if they didn't, I think Aiden would understand if I wanted to spend some time away from court."

"You'd come with me?"

"Are you asking me?"

"Yes?"

I gave him a wry smile. "That didn't sound very convinced. If I'm going with you, I want you to be sure you want me there."

"Then yes. Will you come with me?"

"I'd love to."

Aiden wasn't pleased with my plans to leave so quickly, and less pleased that they involved Joch, but we worked out a compromise. I would stay until his wedding, which was only two months away, on the year anniversary of the

Masquerade where Evie learned she'd fallen in love with a prince. He officially pardoned Joch, but quietly and without any formal proclamations so as not to draw more attention to him. Eventually the people would forget about him and move on, especially with a royal wedding on the horizon.

Mother and Father returned to the palace, looking much healthier and well rested. Aiden was thrilled to give power back to the king, but Father had decided he rather liked not being king anymore. He decided he would return to rule only until Aiden was married, then step down and crown him and Evie the new king and queen.

"Better to show the court you have my support," he'd said. "Especially since you've already begun. It will make the transition smoother when I'm gone."

The wedding was beautiful, and Evie's white mask was one the people would be talking about for years. She'd made it herself and was extremely proud of the elaborate creation. With unlimited access to materials, she'd tastefully arranged diamonds and pearls on the mask. A white opal was on the forehead and two tiny emeralds were at the corners of her eyes as tribute to where she'd come from. White jade hung from silver ornaments in her hair with threads of silver woven into her thick curls.

Aiden was awestruck. He was equally resplendent in his own mask made of clouded glass.

After the wedding, Joch turned to me. "Are you sure you want to leave?"

We'd talked for a long time over what we'd do once we left the palace. Joch's parents lived in the port town and capital city of a country several weeks away, so it was decided that I'd continue my ambassador duties there, strengthening Venesia's ties with the country while Joch reunited with his family and decided what he wanted to do next. When the time came for me to leave, we'd cross that bridge then.

"Venesia is only a place," I told him whenever he protested my leaving the country for him. "I'll always be its princess and there's more than one way for me to serve it."

We didn't know what new adventures would greet us at our destination, but as always, I was optimistic.

Discussion Questions

1. What is the difference between being optimistic and being naive? Which do you think Bianca is?

2. Was Aiden being overprotective or just careful? What would you do if a loved one was in trouble and you were responsible for keeping them safe?

3. What do you think makes a person trustworthy?

4. Do you think Joch deserved forgiveness? Why or why not?

5. Which is more painful: getting hurt yourself or watching someone you care about get hurt?

Acknowledgments

The path to completing this book has been such a rocky one, I barely know where to start.

Thank you to my team at Cedar Fort, especially Emma and Melissa, for having faith I would finish and their endless patience with me.

Thank you to everyone who helped me out behind the scenes. If I tried to name all of you, I would inevitably leave someone out, but I still appreciate every one of you. A special thank you to Jackie and her family for all they did.

As always, thanks to the Internet for better and for worse—plenty of options for research material but also endless distractions.

Thank you to readers that have reached out to me, your enthusiasm and thoughtful comments mean the world to me.

Last, thank you to my family for all their love and support and for being my biggest fans. Aiden would approve.

Photo by Stephanie Staples

Lauren Skidmore grew up in Kansas, with stints in Ohio and New York, and currently lives in Utah. She attended Brigham Young University where she earned a BA in English teaching and minored in Teaching English as a Second Language and Japanese. She then spent a year in Japan teaching and traveling. She hasn't made it to Europe yet, but it's on the list. She has been to thirty states in the United States so far. When she's not exploring new places, you can probably find her on the Internet with fifteen windows open and looking at just one more thing before actually getting something done.

SCAN TO VISIT

WWW.LAURENSKIDMORE.COM